FIRE FINCH

WHEN TOMORROW CALLS

• SERIES •

1. Why You Were Taken (2015)

2. How We Found You (2017)

3. What Have We Done (2017)

ALSO BY JT LAWRENCE

The Memory of Water (2011)

Sticky Fingers (2016)

The Underachieving Ovary (2016)

Grey Magic (2016)

THE SIGMA SURROGATE

JT LAWRENCE

FIRE FINCH
www.firefinchpress.com

The Sigma Surrogate is a work of fiction.

Names, characters, places and incidents are the product of the author's imagination or are used fictitiously. Any resemblance to actual persons, living or dead, events, or locales is entirely coincidental.

2018 Paperback edition

ISBN-13: 978-0-9947234-4-4

1st Edition

Published in South Africa by Fire Finch Press, an imprint of Pulp Books.

www.jt-lawrence.com

Cover photograph from Shutterstock

Set in Bell MT

DEDICATION

This book is dedicated to my readers,
who have changed my life.

Without you I'd be crying into a mug of cheap coffee.

THE SIGMA SURROGATE

THE LUCKY SICKNESS

1

Joni clutches her stomach and hurries towards the Cloisters residence. She tries to swallow the bitter-bright lava climbing up her throat, but she's not going to make it in time.

Flickers of colour perforate her desperation: grass, petals, stones. The smell of moonflowers and compost. Above her, a cloud that looks like a centaur stretches across the sky. She races past the wrought iron gazebo with its fragrant ivory blooms trailing up the sides. Her smart sneakers crunch over the fine cream gravel of the chipstone path, spraying the small pebbles behind her. No doubt the groundswoman will mutter about it later, but Joni doesn't have time to care. Her shoes register her sudden speed and poor traction, and ping a warning to her earbuttons, which she ignores.

A nut-brown rabbit with shining eyes and nervous whiskers hops across her path, and Joni almost stumbles. She knows she shouldn't be running. Too much chance of falling, especially given her curse of eternal clumsiness. Running is Not Allowed here. Falling is Especially Not Allowed.

An unexpected flash of pink at the bottom of a bush catches her eye but she can't stop to look. With her eyes off the path in front of her for that split-second, she trips and her whole body pitches forward.

No no no no. Her body reels in slow motion. Instinct forces her hands out in front of her, and her ivory dress and palms are shredded by the tiny stones as she skids forward on them, saving the rest of her body from the impact.

The sound of the sliding gravel and her shocked breathing is loud in her ears. When she comes to a stop, she stands, places her bleeding hands on her stomach, and gives in to the terrible lurch of the Lucky Sickness.

Her stomach flips and skunky saliva gushes into her mouth. It's too late. She knows by now that when the spit streams like this—a warm sour pool in her mouth—there's no point in running any further. The best thing to do is to stop and grab a paper vombag, which she has, of course, forgotten to bring. Failing that, a bucket or a bin would do. Once, even Mother Blake's favourite yellow coffee mug, the memory of which still shames her, even though she had scrubbed it clean afterwards with bleach and a silver sponge until her hands were raw. She still blushes madly when she sees Blake drink from the thing, thinks she should steal it and smash it instead of being tormented by it every day.

Ridiculous. A smile almost reaches her lips. *Haunted by a coffee mug.*

Then any thought of laughing disappears as her stomach clenches and the vomit jets out of her mouth like an oilrig's lucky day. Joni leans over the perfectly manicured privet hedge and sprays the ground with her gastric juice. Not that there's much in her stomach: water, mostly, and some ginger air wafers that Solonne, the Surrogate Matriarx, had made her eat this morning, promising the fragrant root would help with the nausea. Joni didn't want to eat them, couldn't bear the thought of anything passing her lips, but no one argues with Solonne, especially not in the communal dining room when everyone is watching. Joni had stood at her table like a recalcitrant toddler, chewing the peppery crackers, while the Matriarx nodded at her to keep going. The other SurroSisters had smiled encouragingly, despite their envy of her condition.

Fortunately, the small discs dissolve quickly, even in a dry mouth, and afterwards Joni had been granted a walk in the SurroCloister grounds. Fresh air, and gentle exercise: that was the idea, anyway. Joni vomits again, and this time the acid stings her nose, too. Doubled over, she opens her eyes: Her white gown is scratched and stained by her fall, and the grubbiness is overlaid with fresh crimson blood-handprints, like something out of a horror film. She forces her body up again, and takes a deep breath. Her hands are burning as if she'd slid over hot coals.

Why had no one told her this would be so difficult?

"It will be fun, they said." Joni wipes her mouth and her nose on the back of her hand, muttering away to herself. "It'll be an adventure. You'll be saving the future! It's the most respected job in the country!"

She picks up her copper 'SS' pin that had fallen onto the emerald grass and pins it back over her heart with trembling fingers. She swallows the next heave, and this time it stays down. The worst is over, for now.

It's all kind of true, and the perks *are* awesome, but when you feel this sick for this long, well, no amount of money or respect can really make you feel human. Her body is swollen, her brain is fluff, her mouth is a devil's ashtray.

Gingerly, Joni makes her way back towards the gazebo. She can use the rainwater fountain there to flush away the bitterness and rinse her grazed skin, then she'll head to the matron for some antiseptic plasters and a scolding. The idea of the cool, clean water pushes her reluctant limbs forward. Her smart sneakers ping green: They are happy with her pace now.

We are definitely living in the future, when your shoes double as your nanny.

She sees the flash of pink on the ground again, and this time she stops to look at it.

Oh!

It looks like her fortune is finally turning. At the foot of the hedge, cushioned by a clump of sweet Mexican daisies, is a giant easter egg, most likely left over from the Spring Hunt on Sunday. Easter is always a big deal here. Not the scary Christian version, obviously, but the original Pagan *Ēastre*, celebrating new life and the rite of the northern hemisphere's spring. Even the perennially cross Mother Blake had gotten into the spirit, wearing a crown of chamomile blossoms and diving for choxolate eggs, which had made all the sisters giggle.

The hollow candy egg is the size of an ostrich's, and is made of the palest pink sugar sand, with vintage vanilla lace detail. The scent of imitation strawberry ice cream is subtle, but takes her back in time to when she was a small child. A yapping black poodle, a chintz couch. Sitting on her mother's lap while she knitted blanket squares for the local orphanage. That's when orphanages still existed. Most of Joni's school friends wouldn't even know the word, now. She inhales the comforting scent deep into her lungs. Why is the sense of smell so nostalgic?

Joni holds the delicate egg in her burning, bleeding hands like a hard-won prize. A precious gift from the universe to signal that everything is going to be okay. The Lucky Sickness will pass, she'll be able to complete her job and move back home. Her life will be—relatively—normal again.

Besides, what is normal, nowadays? 2021 is the year of the blight, despite what the UN wants you to believe.

Relentless drought; intractable corporate corruption; the Superbug; the Suicide Contagion. And, of course, the reason she's living in this strange gated community: a devastating infertility crisis. When her over-protective parents told her she'd be safest living here in the Cloister instead of at home, she had railed against them, accused them of abandoning her. But when she glimpses the news headlines on Mother Blake's Tile, or hears the hard-whisper bedtime gossip of the other girls, she knows her parents were right to offer her to the SurroTribe as a recruit.

Even if she had an appetite, Joni decides that the Easter egg is much too pretty to eat. Inspecting its delicate icing, she notices that the egg has a seam: The top and bottom can twist open. There'll be a surprise gift inside. She's torn between seeking the water she's craving and opening the shell. Before she reaches a decision, she swivels the egg, and as it opens she sees a couple of wires attached to something that looks like a battery and some silicone clay, and then there is a loud explosion, and the hot force of it hits Joni in the chest and jaw, and knocks her flat on her back. Joni's last thought, as she lies on the grass, ears chiming, is how very young she is, how short her life has been … and that Solonne will not be very happy. So much for luck.

Drought, crime, suicide, and an Easter egg.

Of all things to be killed by.

She watches the cloud centaur pull back his arrow, and then her vision fades to a blip.

FULL BODY FRISK

2

Keke's on a mission. Five minutes ago she received an anonymous tip-off on a breaking story, and she wants to be the first on the scene. But before that, she has someone to see. Nina, her motorbike, hums between her hot thighs, sending a warm vibration throughout her body. The buildings flitter in her peripheral vision as she expertly leans left and right, left and right, a well-practised slow dance, dodging solar-scooters, potholes, and unpredictable community taxis. The road is shimmering with silver heat. She slows down for a red light, and a military police Hummer rumbles up next to her and winds down the tinted glass.

Hawkers descend on the idling cars, pushing dripping bottles of Hydra through open windows, spraying dirty suds onto windscreens, and showcasing their cheap FongKong multi-shades.

“You in a hurry?” says the cop in the passenger seat.

Kekeletso turns her head to look at him, and sees her reflection in the shiny black bullet-proof duco. She sees what he sees: strong snake-leathered legs hugging the bike, a charcoal kevlar jacket tailored specifically to show off her mahogany-skinned breasts, and the harsh sun glinting off the cat ears of her Neko helmet. The cop has a police-issue tasergun velcro-strapped to his chest and a huge shit-eating grin. Keke knows she'd better answer him, or risk being pulled over for a full-body frisk, or worse—a comprehensive stalk of her record—which is less than sparkling. She doesn't have time for this *kak.*

“I'm talking to you,” the cop says, this time with a hint of neon green venom.

Keke knows she should answer, but instead she looks forward and up at the traffic light—still stubbornly red—and revs her engine.

“Hey!” he says, “I'm talking to you!”

The traffic light flicks to green. The hawkers whistle and jump away from the cars, and Keke twists the grip of her right handlebar forward. Her bike flies full-throttle through the intersection, narrowly missing a red-light-hopping tuktuk. She navigates her way through the gridlock of the next block, and when she's left the Hummer in her dust—

So long, motherfuckers!

—her body relaxes again into the welcoming curves of her bike. The Neko helmet blasts her with cool filtered air and she breathes it in deeply as she roars onto the highway.

She's tracked Kirsten's pixel as being at the MegaMall in Rivonia, although she can't imagine why. Her best friend usually avoids shopping centres like the Superbug. She doesn't understand why creeps would choose to *spend time sucking up other people's breath in fluorescent-lit chambers of capitalism.*

Because you get to buy nice things, Keke always argues. She has no problem dropping bank all over the vanilla floor tiles of any mall. How else would she have found these killer snakeskin leggings?

Online, says the Kirsten in her head.

It's not the same, Keke argues, and then she cuts off the conversation because there's only one thing more absurd than arguing with your best friend, and that's arguing with the phantom of your best friend just before you're about to see her in real life.

She pulls into the vast parking lot of the west zone, close to where Kirsten's pixel is, and comes to a stop in a slender bay with a slowly spinning hologram of a two-wheeler. The hologram disappears as the sensor picks up her bike. She walks towards the entrance, passing a few shoppers laden with bags, including a man wearing a Talking Tee that shouts "Don't drink the water!" that makes Keke jump.

She pulls off her helmet and enters the dim passage to the pedestrian section of the Roller Rink with its rubberised floor. It smells like dirty socks, stale popgrains, spilled CinnaCola, and pink bubble gum. Maraba AfroPop is blasting over the sound system and her pelvis is still humming from riding her bike, giving her a bounce in her step. Keke recognises Kirsten from the back—she'd know that royal red hair anywhere—and she sneaks up behind her, and growls: "What's a nice girl like you doing in a place like this?"

Kirsten starts and spins around, a huge camera in her hands.

"Jesus, Kitty Cat! Careful with that thing!" Keke puts her hands up in mock-defence. "You almost took my head off!"

Kirsten snickers. "Kex! What are you doing here?"

They hug as school-bunking teenagers fly around the rink on laser-skis, hoverboards, airskates and roller-rails. The kids laugh and shout and pull zap signs at each other.

"I came to pick you up." Keke holds up her spare inflatable helmet.

"I'm in the middle of a job," says Kirsten. "Roller Rink Inc."

Keke rolls her eyes. "You used to be cooler, you know that?"

"Really?" says Kirsten.

"Actually, no, not really. But you're not going to want to miss out on this story. My spidey-sense says it's going to be a good one. It might even be The Big One. Wanna tag team?"

Kirsten blinks at her, thinking. Most likely weighing up the nice fat cheque from the mall mafia for today's easy job versus chasing a bare-bones story seed with Keke with no guarantee of anything, except perhaps a criminal record.

"Come on," cajoles Keke, fixing her violet eyes on Kirsten. "You know you want to."

***

"What are you doing?" whispers Kirsten, as Keke leads her around the back of the Conxeption Clinic building. They had parked the bike down the road at a pseudo-sushi bar.

"No way they'll let us in the front," says Keke. "Security at this clinic is tighter than a pole-dancing virgin."

"Ha," says Kirsten. "What do you know about virgins?"

"Less than I know about pole-dancing."

"I thought so. Besides, that analogy makes no sense."

"You might be right," says Keke, "but my point is that your dynap code has to be on the clinic's admission roll to get in, and no one I know could hack the list."

"Because of the short notice?"

"No, because it's fucking iron-clad."

"Yet … you think we'll just be able to waltz in the back door."

"It's the only way. We're rolling old school today. Low tech for the win."

They stand in the shade of a cluster of algaetrees and watch as delivery e-vans arrive and get immediately swallowed up by the cool dark interior of the parking basement. A refrigerated tuk-tuk carrying lab test results, a courier on a Vespa Air, a handsome navy blue limousine.

When a Bilchen catering truck pulls up (*FreshCo. Superfood, Superfast!*), Keke glances at the security guard who yells something friendly but indiscernible at the driver and steps up to inspect the waybill. She grabs Kirsten's hand.

"Now," she says, and they scuttle up to the other side of the truck. The sound of the vehicle's engine disguises their quick footsteps over the hot tarmac, and they slip, undetected, into the heavy shade of the building's basement. The truck continues on to the service bay while Kirsten follows Keke through an avenue of parked cars: super luxurious sedans parked next to old junkers and courier bikes. There'll be plenty of cameras down here.

They reach the blue glass cube of the elevator station, breathing hard, and press the *up* arrow repeatedly to summon the lift, but it doesn't light up. Keke guesses it's a biometric button and kicks the wall.

"We'll have to wait till someone comes down," Kirsten says, "and slip in behind them."

Keke surveys the basement. "We don't have time for that. If any of those cameras registered us we'll be picked up for B&E. We've got a couple of minutes, max."

Kirsten, nervous, finger combs her hair out of her face and spins the ring on her finger. "Maybe we should just get out of here."

What Keke thinks she really means: *I should never have come on this crackers goose chase with you. I should be chilling at the Roller Rink, CinnaCola Crush in hand, counting my blox.*

They study each others' faces as they think, their skin painted luminescent blue, their eyes electric.

Keke can't let her go; she needs Kirsten's help if she's going to crack this one. She knows the tingling sensation in her stomach is a sign to keep going. This story might make her career, and she can't let it get away.

"Hang on," says Keke. "I've got an idea."

The women leave the glass cube behind and head further into the basement, towards the service bay. They reach the back wall and see large square metal doors with symbols embossed on them.

"Utility chutes," says Keke.

Kirsten stops and crosses her arms. "Nope. Nope. Nopity nope nope."

"What?"

"No way I'm climbing up a medical waste chute. Or a

fucking compost chute."

"Where is your sense of adventure?"

"My sense of adventure disappears at the sight of dirty needles and hospital food leftovers."

Keke laughs, Kirsten doesn't.

"I'm not kidding," says Kirsten.

"We're not going up the compost chute," says Keke, wrenching the lever on a different door. A soiled sheet falls to the floor.

Keke motions to Kirsten to start climbing.

"Are you serious?"

"As serious as a heart attack," says Keke.

Kirsten sighs, then jams her dirty sneaker into the lip of the chute, hoists herself up and ducks inside. She stops for a second to look back at Keke. "This story had better be bloody good."

SIGMA

3

Keke and Kirsten climb up the laundry chute. The most difficult part is the smell, which reminds Keke of boarding school, stainless steel canteen breakfasts and being made to kneel on brown sugar. The last bit of the climb is slightly tricky, and Kirsten has to boost Keke so she can crawl through the opening. Then Keke quickly knots and throws down a make-shift linen ladder Kirsten can climb.

Once in the laundry room, they search through dirty lab coat pockets, trying to find forgotten ID chips or keycards, but come up empty-handed. They spot some freshly laundered medical aprons and masks in the cabinets and sneak into a surgeon's sleep pod to pull them on.

Keke locks the door, then drops to the floor and looks under the swingbed.

"Ha!" she says, triumphant, and pulls out a pair of charcoal satin panties.

"These pods are never really used for actual sleeping, are they?" says Kirsten.

"I don't think so."

Keke reaches even further under the bed and pulls out a lanyard with an ID card and an access chip.

"Bingo!" says Kirsten, and Keke laughs.

Kirsten frowns. "What?"

"*Bingo,*" says Keke, chuckling. "You do realise that only people who live in old movies and retirement villages use that word, right?"

Kirsten blushes.

Keke feels a wave of affection for her best friend and smacks her on the arm. "You're adorable. Ancient, but adorable."

Keke shrugs off her leather jacket and Kirsten stares at her shoulder. "Time for a shot?"

Keke looks down at her insulin-sensitive white ink tattoo. The antique lace illustration is showing off beautifully on her dark skin. "Shit."

She'd been so focused on breaking in here she had forgotten to bring her insulin, which is in her clamshell, safe in the stowaway of her bike.

"We need to hurry."

They walk down the Conxeption Clinic's corridor in their

stolen scrubs. Luckily, there are plenty of people around, and they blend in easily. *East wing*, her snitch had said. Keke thinks she'll have to pickpocket someone's Tile to find a room number but then they see a huge glass notice board that keeps ticking over with updates on patient information. More like a flight schedule at a Volanter airport than a fertility clinic.

"I can't believe how big this place is." There's a look of pale desolation on Kirsten's face.

"Sorry," says Keke. "This can't be easy for you."

Kirsten had been dragged from one specialist to another when she was a child. She was continually prodded and x-rayed and scanned and pricked as her parents searched for a diagnosis for her synaesthesia. No wonder doctors creeped her out. And the fact that Conxeption is a fertility clinic just makes it worse, given Kirsten's current obsession to conceive.

Keke has never understood the urge to have children; she wasn't born with the breeding gene. The idea of broodiness puzzles her, and the thought of having a small human depend on her is nothing less than terrifying. She can't even keep a plant alive, never mind a mewling baby. And small kids are even worse. They drink drain cleaner and climb on skyscraper windowsills and go off with strangers. They're way too unpredictable, and Keke has more than enough of that in her life. Still, she feels for Kirsten. She knows what it's like to crave something so intimate.

"What's her name?" whispers Kirsten.

"What?" asks Keke, but then she snaps back to the moment.

"The victim's name?"

"I don't know."

The board keeps clicking over. 226 patients and counting.

"You don't know?"

"My snitch didn't say, and they won't release her name. They're trying to keep the whole thing under the Blanket."

Keke studies the ticking glass board. "She would have been brought in this morning, between nine and ten. She'll be in Casualty or A&E or something like that. It's not like she's here for regular fertility treatment."

Keke's not sure why the victim is here at all, instead of at a real hospital with real trauma doctors.

They look at the various wards: Consulting; Labs; Counselling; Surgery; Retrieval; Transfers; Care.

Keke sees Kirsten shudder. No matter how badly she wants to get pregnant, she won't agree to IVF. She doesn't want to 'force it' she says, but Keke doesn't understand why she resists the science. If it weren't for medicine, Keke thinks, picturing her tattoo pulsing under her stolen scrubs, she wouldn't be alive.

"Care," says Kirsten.

"Yes, that sounds right."

"One patient admitted just before ten. No name. Just that symbol."

Ward CARE 9:58 Room 6A Σ

"Sigma," says Keke.

"What-what?"

"Sigma. It's the eighteenth letter of the Greek alphabet. It means the sum of everything."

"It sounds like the name of a sorority house."

"You're getting warm."

"What?"

"Where she comes from … it's kind of like a sorority house. Except not really. Not at all."

"You're babbling. I think we should go find you some insulin."

"Nonsense. Just remember '6A'."

"That's easy," says Kirsten, who has a photographic memory. "Pink Lemonade."

"Now who's babbling?"

"6A. Six is pink. 'A' is pale yellow, with a bit of fizz. A fine spray of dots. Pink Lemonade."

Keke shakes her head. Sometimes she thinks her best friend is living in a different reality altogether. She's sure that if her sensory brain wires were crossed like Kirsten's are, she'd never be able to get anything done.

"Don't say it," says Kirsten. "I know what you're thinking. I'm adorable."

They make their way to the east wing, using the chip card to unlock any obstacles, and find room 6A. Keke stands on her toes to look through the small glass window, but still can't see much. Sometimes being petite has its disadvantages. Kirsten, a head taller, has a better view.

"Is she alone?" whispers Keke, and Kirsten nods.

Keke looks from side to side, unlocks the door, and they both slip in.

PALE AS PAPER

4

Keke presses the stolen access card up to the ward door and the lock clicks open. The women slip into the dim room and tiptoe up to the bed. A slender sleeping body lies under the covers. Patient Sigma is wearing a white gauze mask and her hands are bandaged. She's hooked up to an IV and a heart rate monitor, and her blood-flecked honey hair is spread over the white cotton pillowcase. Keke uses her phone to soundlessly scan her medical file.

There is a sound at the door, and Kirsten looks at Keke as if to say *Have you got what you need?* and Keke mouths *Almost.* She looks around for something that might have the patient's fingerprint on it, but the room is minimalist to the max: It doesn't even seem to have a bin. Kirsten motions to hurry, and Keke is about to give up on the fingerprint when her SugarApp rings with a warning to take her insulin: a submarine ping. The patient stirs.

Sigma's eyes click open, bright with fear, and she grabs the hospital bed rails with her bandaged hands. Tries to sit up, but can't. "Who are you?"

F-u-u-u-ck.

Should Keke lie? Say they're here to take her lunch order? Lying is one of Keke's many talents.

The patient smacks her remote, and Keke expects an alarm to sound, but instead the lights flicker on above them, throwing them all into sharp detail. Kirsten is as pale as paper.

"Who are you?" the patient asks again. Warm white knuckles on cold steel.

"We're friends," says Keke.

"That's not an answer." She presses another button on the remote and the bed levers her up into a sitting position. The cotton sheet that had been covering her torso falls to her lap, revealing bandaged shoulders and breasts, and a sensor strapped to her stomach.

"You're pregnant," says Kirsten, not hiding her surprise.

Tears well up in the surrogate's eyes. She puts her wrapped palms up to her face, and rests the heels of her hands on her closed eyelids. When her fingers touch the gauze they spring away in revulsion, then go back to explore the foreign texture. Soon she starts peeling off the mask.

"Don't," says Kirsten, but it's too late. The gauze comes

away easily and they see the raw bloody damage on her forehead and cheeks, stitched, and shiny with some kind of ointment residue.

Keke almost winces at what she sees, but tries to keep her expression even. Just looking at the surrogate's burnt and lacerated skin makes her own face sting. Anger starts to smoke inside her.

The patient searches the walls for a mirror but there is none. Keke reluctantly offers her phone's Mirror app, and the patient studies her new reflection without reacting.

"Who did this to me?"

"That's what we're here to find out."

She starts sniffing, and Kirsten passes her a tissue from a box on the windowsill.

"It's my fault," she says.

"This is *not* your fault," says Keke, moving a step closer, and surreptitiously pocketing a piece of bandage from the bed.

"It is. I was complaining this morning about the job. About the Lucky Sickness. I was kind of wishing that I wasn't pregnant anymore, that I wasn't a surrogate."

"That sounds perfectly reasonable to me," says Keke. "Being pregnant can't be easy. Especially when you're doing it for someone else."

Kirsten moves closer to her. "You're worried about the baby?"

"I have a bad feeling," cries the surrogate. "A very bad feeling."

"What did the doctors say?"

"They said the baby's fine. They're monitoring us closely." They all look at the machines at the same time, and see the reassuring scribble of the foetal heart monitor. "But that blast ... how could a b-baby survive that?"

"Tell us what happened."

Sigma hesitates, then her shoulders drop and she starts to talk. "I was walking in the garden, and I found an easter egg. A poisoned Easter egg."

Kirsten frowns. "Poisoned?"

"Booby-trapped," says Keke. "In VR games and sim training a booby trap masquerading as a bonus pick-up is called a poisoned Easter egg. We're not talking about actual poison. Obviously."

"But it was an actual Easter egg," says the patient. "A beautiful one."

Keke narrows her eyes as she thinks. Who would try to hurt a SurroSister? They're the most respected people in the country.

"Do you have any enemies?" asks Kirsten, and the Surro shakes her head.

"No. I mean, a few of my school friends were envious when I was recruited by the Tribe, but I've never had an enemy in my life."

Keke and Kirsten lock eyes. *Not until now.*

"What are you doing in here?" says a voice from behind them, and they all jump.

"Mother Blake," says the surrogate, her voice wobbly from crying. "I didn't hear you come in."

A large, matronly woman in Senior Surro get-up strides into the room. Her copper pin has been polished to within an inch of its life, and it shines aggressively in their direction.

"Who the hell are you? How did you get in here?" says the woman to the interlopers. "I'm calling security!"

"No." Kirsten steps backwards. "It's not necessary. We're leaving."

Blake slams something on her Tile. "Too late!" she booms. "They're on their way."

She gives them both a pointed look, and her short-cropped black hair clings to her damp temples.

"You should be ashamed of yourselves, coming in here, upsetting a Surro."

"They didn't," says Sigma, her battered face still shining with tincture and tears.

Blake spots Kirsten's locketcam. "I knew it. You're with the press."

The surrogate looks horrified. She pulls the sheet up around her neck.

"Well," says Keke, "we are, but—"

"You cannot publish this story," says Blake. "You cannot."

"What is the story?" asks Keke.

A clinic security guard arrives, and Keke and Kirsten steel themselves for their forced removal, but instead he taps politely on the door and sticks his head in. "Problem?"

The muscles in Blake's jaw ripple as she clenches her teeth. She doesn't take her eyes off Keke. "I don't know yet."

"I'll wait outside," he says, and closes the door again.

"What's going on?" asks Keke. "Why would anyone—"

"It's none of your business," says Blake.

"When a surrogate gets attacked it's everyone's business," says Keke. "How did they get into the Cloister? I've seen those drawings of the compound. It's airtight."

Blake doesn't answer; she just stares at Keke with flaring nostrils.

"Inside job?" Kirsten wonders aloud.

"Never!" says Blake. "That would never happen."

Keke angles her head, thinking. "They screen the fucking daylights out of anyone before granting access."

"Then someone broke in?"

"Impossible," says Blake.

Keke crosses her arms. "Apparently not."

Blake sighs and rests her hands on the metal rail at the end of the bed. "Look. We are busy with our own investigation."

"Really?"

"Once we have more information we'll make a statement to the press."

Keke purses her lips. *I've heard that before.*

"Our main focus at the moment is to look after the sisters, especially our patient here. She's still in shock. And she certainly isn't supposed to be exposed to any additional stress." Blake gestures towards the foetal heart rate monitor. "If you won't leave on my accord, then do it for the baby."

Damn it. Keke can't argue with that. Plus, her mouth feels desiccated, and she's starting to feel the pins and needles of her too-high blood sugar. They need to get out of here, but Keke doesn't give up that easily. She stands her ground, crosses her arms.

Blake sighs. "If you leave quickly and quietly I'll tell the guard to stand down."

"Grant us access to the Cloister," says Keke.

Blake looks genuinely shocked. "You can't be serious."

"Let us help with the investigation."

"Keke's super connected," says Kirsten. "Believe me, you want her on your side."

"I think we've got it covered without you adding to our trouble," says Blake, opening the door for them. "And the very last thing I need are the cyber paparazzi buzzing around where they don't belong. Now, get lost, before I get you both arrested."

Kirsten takes a step, but Keke's reluctant to leave. She needs to question the Surro. She's strangely drawn to the girl, perhaps because she looks so vulnerable there against the starched white linen. Keke feels protective of her. How old is she? Seventeen? Too young to be cut off from family like this—Keke severed ties with her own family at fifteen, so she should know—and way too young to be pregnant, but that's how the Surros roll. They have to recruit members as young as possible without breaking the law. Fertility starts plummeting at nineteen and that's not a risk they can take, not in a country where less than one percent of the population is fertile. Not unless they want an old age dystopia on their hands, with no young guns to do the work and prop up the economy. Someone's got to grind to pay for the wheelchairs and adult diapers. The Fertile Myrtles need to be snatched up as soon as possible and put to work—or bedrest, or whatever it is that pregnant surrogates do—before their eggs turn grey and grizzled like the rest of the population's.

And if those all-important surrogates get targeted, it'll be a bleak future indeed. Everyone in the country has a stake in this, and Keke's sure that's why she's got that tingling feeling. This story has the potential to be the feature of the year. They start moving towards the door, and Sigma looks totally bereft. There's no way Keke can leave without giving her some kind of hope of closure. As it is, her aura of desolation seeks to drown Keke where she stands.

Fuck it. I'm running with this piece, no matter what. This girl deserves justice, the SurroTribe deserves to feel safe, and I deserve this story.

"Whether or not the Tribe approves," she says to the Surro, giving Blake a sidelong glance, "We're going to find out who did this to you."

FLOWERGRRL

5

Keke's motorcycle pulls up with a roar outside Jasmine's wildly cultivated property. The security gate slides open smoothly for her, and she parks inside, her tyres crushing some peppery-smelling ground cover with tiny purple blooms. She kicks down the stand and hops off, lifting her Neko helmet and stowing it under the seat. When she looks up, Jasmine is standing outside her caravan, watching her. Keke, buzzing from the ride here, wants to rip Jasmine's clothes off, but she holds back. Best to first take care of business.

"FlowerGrrl," Keke growls.

"I love it when you call me that."

The plants around them sway sweetly in the warm afternoon breeze. There's not an inch of barren soil. Keke touches a lime green lily with a lightning bolt for a stamen. Electric Lily, Kirsten might say, if she were here. Kirsten would go crazy for this place. She has an almost unhealthy obsession of plants, and her flat in Illovo is a veritable jungle. Keke admires the view as she approaches Jasmine, and the flowers' perfume sings.

"You've been busy."

"You know me," says Jasmine. "I like to keep my hands occupied." A naughty silver spark in her eyes makes Keke's pelvis thrum. "Come inside."

Keke follows Jasmine into her caravan, admiring her waist from behind, cinched by a copper corset, and the glinting rivets in her beehive hair. Victorian illustrations are etched in ink on her pale skin. The woman knows how to make steampunk sexy.

The caravan is completely modded out. It's like Vincent van Gogh and Henry Ford got it on and had a pet project love child they covered in cogs and hammered copper plates. Keke sometimes teases Jasmine, asking her when she'll make the thing fly. She imagines it growing giant vellum dragon wings and flapping away into the horizon.

But Jasmine doesn't have time for such flights of fancy. She's a steampunk tinker, a gene-hacking florist, and the head of Alba: a biopunk organisation of hacktivists who work to expose dodgy clinics and evil corps. Keke met her through her darkweb contacts, a network of truthers who open-source with each other, giving or trading information, to fight the Evil.

Keke knows evil doesn't come in the form of devils or curses. Evil is one hundred percent human, and it's their job to fight it. Alba, and other organisations like it, along with individual warriors such as her, work to do what they can to stem the tide of toxic corporate vice and political corruption. Most of the time the data they scrape is shared freely. Sometimes it's traded for gaming currency, bioware, or sex. Keke's relationship with Jasmine didn't start out this way, but the day they met—to exchange some grey-market spyware—it was as if they were both hit by lightning. They wanted each other immediately.

"Do you remember the day we met?" asks Keke.

Jasmine pauses in setting up her bespoke printer and looks up. "Of course."

It's then when Keke sees her fingers, and frowns. "Did you hurt yourself?"

Jasmine looks down at her spark plasters. "Oh! No."

Keke steps forward and kisses Jasmine's fingertips.

"I'm not hurt. This is my latest invention. I'm still testing it out."

She snaps her fingers three times, then a spark appears, and a flame.

"Whoah! That's cool."

Jasmine holds the flame for a moment longer, then blows it out.

Those lips.

"Like magic," says Keke.

"Better than magic," says Jasmine, and winks at her. She turns on the printer. "Did you bring the girl's fingerprint?"

"I couldn't get it. One of the Senior Surros bust us."

"Shit!"

"But not before I got this." Keke pulls a clear plastic bag out of her leather jacket pocket. Inside is a bandage, brown with blood.

"Oh, very good."

Jasmine reaches for a shelf above her and brings down a DNA kit. She snaps on some red cinnamon biolatex gloves and gets to work, clipping a small piece of bandage and swirling it in a high-tech test tube with a squirt of clear liquid, which she then clips into the printer. A holoscreen appears.

Joni Mielke, it says, and lists the injured surrogate's genetic profile code in a 3D barcode.

"What do you need?" Jasmine asks. "Fingerprints?"

"Yes. And irises, if you can."

"I can."

Jasmine inputs the code, and the screen turns from blue to green.

"Okay, that's good news. It's read the DNA and successfully fetched the dynap code. Thundercats are go."

"God, you're sexy when you work," says Keke.

Jasmine ignores her, keeping her attention squarely on the printer as it begins to hum. A minute later, three small slips of paper arrive in the tray. Jasmine picks them up and slides them into a small plastic sleeve.

"Have you used silicone fingerprints before?"

"No," says Keke.

"They're basically just stickers. You peel one off and stick it onto your own finger. I printed three for you, just in case."

Keke studies the silicone pattern, with a whorl like an opening bloom.

Next the printer releases two more slips.

"And these work exactly like contact lenses. Peel them off, like the prints, and add a little saline."

Keke knows how to put in lenses. Part of her look is her bright violet eyes, which are not her natural colour. Lens technology fascinates her. She's recently pledged ten thousand Blox to a startup in the Cape Republic working on smart lenses that can dispense insulin according to constant blood sugar readings. She loves her tattoo, but she won't miss the shots.

"I'm still working on the formula of the lenses," says Jasmine. "It's not perfect. The iris pattern begins to degrade after an hour or so of being inserted, so whatever you have to do, make it quick."

"Thank you so much," says Keke, pocketing the prints and the irises.

"You're very welcome." Jasmine blinks her extreme lashes at her. "Quid pro quo?"

"Of course. What can I do for you?"

"A little bird told me you have a story for me."

Keke's confused at first. She's been so focused on the Sigma Surrogate story that everything else in the periphery of her mind seems to have faded to almost nothing. But then she remembers. It was something she had 'overheard' in an online chatroom via a new cyberspy application she's been trying out. She can't place any stock in it yet. One rumour does not a story make.

"It's not a story. Not yet. It's not even the start of a story."

"Tell me."

"It's just a locker room rumour."

"My favourite! Whose locker room?"

"Give me one more day to triangulate. I don't want to send you on a wild goose chase."

Jasmine looks disappointed.

"All right."

"If it works out, you'll be the first and only to get it, I promise. I think it'll be perfect for you."

"Okay. I'll try to be patient."

"In the mean time," says Keke, reaching out for the buttons on Jasmine's dress, "I have other ways to thank you."

Keke pops the buttons open slowly, expertly, with one hand. A rose-skin blush ascends Jasmine's ivory throat. She bites her lip. Keke turns her around, nuzzles the back of her neck, and unclips her warm metal corset. She lowers it to the floor, and she stays there, on her knees, lifting the skirt of Jasmine's dress and kissing and nipping the back of her thighs. Jasmine steps out of the corset and leans over the counter, allowing Keke the perfect view of the back of her thighs. They are pale, and perfect, and where they meet at the top, under Jasmine's russet bronze panties, makes Keke's stomach flip with naked desire. Keke reaches for Jasmine's thighs again, kisses her harder, uses her tongue now, too, working her way up the creamy skin towards the apex, and Jasmine groans. Before she reaches it, she stops to admire Jasmine's peach of an ass. Keke's pulsating, a deep vibration is running right through her, as if her pelvis is a giant bell that's been rung.

"My god I want you." Keke's voice is thick with her craving for Jasmine, who groans again as Keke keeps climbing.

"Don't stop," Jasmine says, and Keke doesn't.

DO NOT ANGER THE A.I. GODS

6

Keke leaves her motorbike under the shade of an old oak and walks the last few hundred metres to the entrance of the gated community of the SurroCloister. The double walls are smooth and high—impossible to climb, even with a grappling hook. Silver micro-glitter in the white enamel makes the surface sparkle. Keke feels the heat of the wall as she strides past it.

When she nears the entrance, she slows, adjusts the foreign clothes. She hopes she's got the walk right: quietly confident, purposeful, no swagger. She's got the outfit right: She picked up a Surro gown from a costume hire shop whose assistant swore the design was identical to the real thing, down to the slightly weighted hem, the underarm air vents, and the pearlescent shoulder caps. She's wearing a pale straw hat, nondescript white leggings, and white sneakers. A milky silk scarf. The only item of her ensemble that's missing is the coveted copper 'SS' pin. Keke had tried to buy one on the MarXet, but not even the usual greyware creeps dare stock it. It's a criminal offence to sell, copy, or illicitly possess the pin. And, jail-time aside, it's just looked down upon by most, even those who don't have a problem selling spike or heat. They'd risk getting slung into a penal labour colony for white lobster and/or firepower, but not for a copper pin.

Keke reaches the entrance, gives a subtle nod of sunhat and sunglasses towards the guard on duty, and approaches the pedestrian gate. She says a quick nonsense prayer to whichever gods happen to be trending, and puts her thumb onto the scanner of the biometric access pad. She's one hundred percent confident in Jasmine's biohacking abilities but her nerves stab at her, regardless. What if her perspiration dislodges the silicone fingerprint? What if her printed lenses have already started to dissolve? Despite her anxiety, she tries to remain relaxed in case the guard is watching her.

Of the two red lights on the access pad, one turns green. Next, she looks forward, into the retina scanner, and lifts her shades. The second light changes to green, and the gate gives a friendly beep, clicks open, and Keke feels a splash of cool relief as she enters the grounds and closes the gate behind her.

Her relief is immediately clouded over by a sense of foreboding with the realisation that with enough tech in your arsenal, it *is* possible to break into the Cloister. So much for it being impenetrable.

This is not good news.

The number of potential suspects just ramped up exponentially.

A few years ago, the architectural plans for the compound were leaked online. There was an uproar—the public were anxious about the SurroSisters' subsequent safety—but the plans revealed that the security of the Cloister was airtight, and the leak was sure to put off anyone even thinking of trying to break in. There was even a political satire cartoon about it, published by Echo.news: something about the amusing irony of a surrogate compound being impregnable. At the time Keke had wondered if the leak was done on purpose—an inside job—a strategy to show any would-be interlopers that breaking in would be impossible, and stop them in their tracks.

Well, it worked. For a while, anyway.

It had worked for years, but now the Surros are at risk. Who would want to harm a surrogate in the first place? A religious nut? A bitter recruit reject? An estranged boyfriend? Joni didn't seem like the type to have a possessive lover at home. In fact, Keke would be surprised if Joni has ever had a boyfriend. She seems like a Good Girl, with that wholesome, honey-coloured hair and clear blue eyes. A beautiful face, Keke assumes, before the attack. Virtuous. A daughter to be proud of. Keke's never been any of those things. In fact, inside and outside, Joni seems to be her polar opposite, and yet she feels a connection to the girl she can't shake.

Keke's scarf starts to strangle her. It's too hot, too tight. She loosens it, even though it means that more of her face and neck are visible.

She lopes up the concrete paving, a long, uphill path that snakes its way through short-cropped grass and water-wise, indigenous gardens: purple-feathered grasses and happy succulents. As she reaches the top of the hill, the main building comes into view: a beautiful post-modern design—a giant, super-stylised lotus flower. Beyond the rear boundary wall, wind turbines are planted as far as the eye can see. The wind farm supplies the Cloister, as well as the surrounding area, and feeds back into the alt-grid. Not that the Cloister needs it with all the solar trees gleaming in the morning light. Keke increases her pace, her eyes on the main building.

The petals of the lotus move in accordance to the sun. They close up during hot days like this, to keep the interior cool and shaded, and as soon as the temperature drops, the building blooms, pushing its petals outwards and down, its petals reflecting the white light of the moon.

Keke's not going to even try to get into the Lotus. What she's after is in the security hub.

Her heart jigs. She's always been so curious as to what it was like inside here, and never believed she'd get to see it. It's far quieter than she imagined. Where are all the SurroSisters? Perhaps they're resting in the dorms, or busy with their lessons.

The Surro Matriarx, Solonne, believes that the young women need to be kept busy, so she maintains a demanding schedule of lessons and activities. There's a menu to choose from, but Keke has heard that they learn, amongst other things, coding, kung-fu, Blox trading, horseback-riding, and archery. Of course, this is only till they conceive. Pregnant Surros are afforded the very best of everything—a reward for renting out their wombs to save the population from tanking—including long days of rest and delicious food, and leisurely walks in the beautifully landscaped surroundings, under the watchful eyes of the white security cam drones.

When Keke's in a nihilistic mood, she wonders why everyone is so desperate to reverse the infertility crisis. Surely there's a reason that creeps have stopped having children? The health goths will tell you that the earth will recover once humans are wiped off the planet. It'll take hundreds of years, but it will recover. Like someone with the Black Lung who stops vaping, and stops breathing in the city pollution. The plants will creep over everything, and the endangered animals will breed, and the earth won't explode from sheer fuckery like it seems to want to do, with all the abuse we're aiming at it. Sure, Mother Nature gets us back every now and then. A tornado here, a tsunami there, but what we really need is a catastrophe of vast proportions, something that'll wipe out most of the human population.

Or, Keke thinks cheerfully, *a plague.*

We're long overdue for an epidemic, aren't we?

There's the Suicide Contagion, of course. That seems to be gathering momentum. No one has figured out yet why all of a sudden finding novel ways to snuff yourself is on trend. Everyone's doing it. The barista who used to serve Keke her coffeeberry shooter without her having to say a word; Jasmine's hotpunk hairdresser; the creepy guy down the passage from Kitty's apartment who used to smell of blunt and sour socks. Kirsten calls the Suiciders 'the lemmings', which makes Keke snort. They've always shared a dark sense of humour.

What can you do but laugh? Kirsten joked the other day, *when life hands you lemmings?*

Someone walks out of the Lotus building, so Keke puts her head down and keeps moving. The woman is wearing the same uniform as she is, so Keke guesses she's a SurroSister. God, Keke would love to spend a week in here, observing the inner machinery and how it works, speaking to the surrogates. She'd do anything to be granted an in-depth piece here. Soon there's another woman in white, and another, bright against the emerald carpet of grass, as if they are being cloned before Keke's eyes—a glitch in the Matrix—but then Keke realises they've probably just finished a class.

The security cam drones come out too, and hover around the surrogates like giant white wasps.

"Hey!" comes a masculine shout from behind her. The security guard. Keke freezes.

Shit!

"Hey!" he shouts, and Keke takes a breath and spins around. What's the maximum sentence for breaking into the SurroCloister?

Ten years.

Breathe.

Breathe.

She turns around to look at him.

"You dropped something!" he yells, using his hands as a loudspeaker, and then points at the ground between them.

So he *had* been watching her. Keke looks at the path and sees she's dropped her white scarf. Her nerves are making her sloppy.

Fuck! Calm the fuck down and be more careful.

She waves at the guard and swoops to pick it up, noticing for the first time that the grass is not organic. It's that SuperNatural astroturf—a no-brainer, really, given the drought—but the knowledge makes Keke feel strangely uncomfortable. Perhaps because it took her so long to notice it wasn't real. Perhaps because it's making her wonder what else is not what it seems, here in the heart of Surroland.

A security drone catches sight of Keke, and speeds towards her. She quickly adjusts her hat and looks down, hoping to obscure her face. She winds the scarf around her chin and neck again and hurries along the path, breathing fast, and the drone finally loses interest and flies away.

The path leads to the women's residence, then forks to the main garden, the sports fields, and the stables. Keke follows the way to the dorms but then leaves the path to get to the back of the plain slab of a building. Unless they've redesigned the layout, the security hub is a small room next to the kitchen.

As she creeps closer, Keke hears the clashing of stainless steel cooking implements and smells that distinct cafeteria odour. *Canteen Vomitous*, she used to call it. She's assailed by a hundred micro-memories of her time at boarding school, most of them pretty shitty. Conservative hostel mistresses who side-eyed you for having an opinion, for having writing talent, for having a great set of tits. Having curves was a daily outrage.

That's probably why schoolmarm-ish Mother Blake gives her the creeps.

Keke shudders.

Prickly bed sheets. Thin mattresses. Ready-made hot drinks in simmering urns that were so weak you couldn't tell whether it was tea or coffee or just plain dirty water. And the awful food. *Ai*, the food. No wonder most of the girls ended up putting on a kilogram a term, because the only way to escape the deep and gnawing hunger was to hoard a stack of CaraCrunch bars under your pillow.

There were some good memories too. Not many, but she

does remember some highlights. Walking to town on autumn days, arm in arm with other schoolgirls. Long afternoons spent reading under a giant plane tree. Sharing shower time slots with hostel mates, ostensibly to get a longer shower, but for Keke it was more about the intimacy of the event. Warm blasts of water, big soft sponges and suds, and all that beautiful young nakedness on display. Sometimes they would kiss. The other girls would call it 'practice'. They were 'practising' for when they got to kiss boys. But for Keke it was always the real thing. Her constant gnawing hunger wasn't for food; she was born with a different kind of appetite. She'd lose herself in those hot, wet kisses. Tongues and fingers and slippery skin. Some of the girls wondered if that pleasure meant they were gay or bi. Keke never worried about finding a box to fit in; she'd known she was ambisextrous long before it became fashionable.

Keke shakes the distracting thoughts from her head.

What is wrong with me today?

She's totally off her game. It's like the weirdness of the Cloister and what happens here is leaking into her brain. She needs to get out of her head and focus on the task at hand. She slips into the shade of the building behind the kitchen, and makes her way to the door on the other side. Of course, it's locked, as she knew it would be. She walks back along the perimeter and tries the kitchen door, which is open. She sneaks in, careful to close the door quietly behind her. Two women are dressed in catering garb and hairnets, fussing over a platter under the warming lamp, and another who is sweating through her apron, pushing a heap of soy sausages around in a giant pan. The noisy sizzle of the schmeat masks Keke's footsteps as she scuttles, bent over, along the back of the kitchen, and through the dining room door. From there she winds back towards the hub: through a short passage and left, until she sees the door she's looking for. This one is slightly ajar, and she's able to peek inside, and see that the desk is unmanned. The security hub is monitored by artificial intelligence, so it's not necessary to have a dozing human watching the cameras with their eyes shut. Any unusual activity would send a red flag directly to the security company and they'd go on immediate lockdown.

Do not trip a red flag, thinks Keke, who can hear her heart beating now. *Do not anger the AI gods.*

As she surveys the room and its equipment, she can smell the frying soy and it makes her stomach turn. The sooner she gets out of here, the better. She retrieves her Xdrive from the tongue of her left sneaker, finds the entry point on the humming machine in the centre of the room, and slots it in. Male into female. Isn't it funny how everything always comes back to sex? Or at least, it does for her, anyway.

She quickly types in the list of commands she's learnt by heart, and the information starts copying across. She doesn't know exactly what she's looking for, so she copies the entire year's data. All the videos, documents and communication with a timestamp of 2021 flits into her drive. She can still hear her heart smashing away. Why is she so damn nervy? Must be a combination of the prospect of the crim colony if she gets caught, the memories of hostel, and worry about Joni.

The data transfer is at seventy-eight percent when she

hears voices coming towards her.

Shit.

She looks for somewhere to hide, but the room is so poky there really is nowhere to conceal herself. She can't pull the drive out yet without corrupting the transfer. She dives under the desk and hugs her knees to her chest, making herself as small as possible. If they pass by, no one will spot her, but if someone decides to come around to this side of the machine they'll see her immediately. The voices get louder.

Shit. Shit, shit, shit.

The repulsive smell of the kitchen is replaced by the scent of Keke's stress-sweat.

Ten years in a PLC.

Ten years locked up in an institution eleventy thousand times worse than a stuffy boarding school.

Ten years sewing superbug face masks or fracking oil or stuffing fucking soy sausages. What was I thinking? No story is worth that.

The chatting women pause at the doorway. Keke swallows hard, squeezes her eyes closed, and waits to be discovered.

FIVE MINUTES TO FREEDOM

7

The women, still chatting, move away from the doorway, allowing Keke to take a deep breath.

Christ on a cracker, that was close.

If only she could stop her heart from jackhammering in her ears. Keke jumps up and retrieves her Xdrive, attaches it to her sneaker again. She looks up and down the passage, and, seeing it's clear, takes the gap. Back towards *Canteen Vomitous,* back towards the path that will deliver her outside the grounds and to precious Nina, the sexiest motorbike in the southern hemisphere. She manages to sneak through the back of the kitchen as before. The cooks are serving lunch now, so Keke doesn't even have to duck while she runs.

Before she takes a step into the welcome fresh air, she quickly checks her outfit, straightens her dress, adjusts her scarf, puts her sunglasses and hat back on. Tries to relax her face even though she is seriously on edge.

Just five minutes to freedom, she thinks, as she begins walking back to the main entrance, when she's stopped by a whistling white arrow that narrowly misses her chest and plunges into the wall next to her.

What the—

Keke ducks and runs, but the attacker fires off another arrow and it flies so close to her cheek she can hear the universe in it. She stops and raises her hands.

"Don't shoot!"

The SurroSister approaches, arrow pointed directly at Keke's torso, the string of her bow ratcheted up to such a high tension it's practically singing.

"Are you crazy?" demands Keke. "You could have killed me."

The surrogate does have a bit of a crazy look in her eye. A smile twitches at her lips.

"I've never scored less than ten," she says, which makes Keke think she must be a psychopath. Did other serial killers boast to their victims about their accuracy?

"Congratulations," says Keke. "Your parents must be proud."

The woman laughs and lowers her weapon. Keke takes in

her flowing white robe, her strong arms, like some Greek goddess superhero redux.

"You've chosen a very bad time to break into the Cloister," says the surrogate.

"How do you know I broke in?" asks Keke. "That I'm not a new sister? In fact, wouldn't it be irresponsible of you to shoot an arrow at someone who may be a new addition to your tribe?"

"You're not a member of our tribe," says the woman, casting a pointed look at Keke's chest, bare of the copper 'SS' brooch. "I could tell from a mile off. In normal circumstances I would have given you the benefit of the doubt, but..."

"But it's not normal circumstances," says Keke. "After the blast yesterday."

"Yes."

"I understand that you're taking extra precautions," says Keke. "But I'm not here to do any harm. On the contrary—"

The SurroSister angles her head at Keke, as if trying to work out if she's telling the truth.

"I'm here to help. I spoke to Joni. After the attack."

"You didn't."

"I did."

"The Sigma case is sealed. No one knows her identity. Not even the doctors know her real name."

"Well. I don't want to boast, but—"

The woman's eyes, bright with suspicion, dart all over, then home in on Keke's blue lenses, which are probably already fading.

"How did you get into her room at the clinic?" she demands. "How did you get in *here*?"

"I have my ways."

"Come with me."

"I'd rather not."

"I'm taking you to Mother Blake. She can decide what to do with you."

"No. I'm going to make a hasty exit, and you're going to tell the Powers That Be that you couldn't stop me from leaving. That's if you have to tell them anything at all."

The woman snorts. Her large face is attractive, but her personality taints the prettiness.

"Even if I let you go, they won't let you out the front gate. I sounded the silent alarm. We're on lockdown."

Keke looks around. The vast property is now empty of the multiplying Surros.

The archer clenches her jaw. "You're coming with me, or I'll put an arrow between your shoulder blades as you walk away, got it?"

Keke searches the sister's mean face for signs of bluffing.

She can't see any. Still, she has to take the chance, because there's no way she can risk being detained and arrested. She starts walking in the direction of the entrance, but with each step her feet become heavier with dread.

Keke hears the bow being drawn again, and the arrow moving against the wood, and she can almost feel the sting of the sharp bolt piercing her back, as if it's happened already in a parallel life that runs just a second faster than this one. Surely the surrogate won't harm her? Keke keeps walking, breathing, trying to push down the panic bleeding into her stomach. Just as she senses a glimmer of hope that she'll make it outside, she hears a high zing and feels a searing lighting bolt in her back, and falls face-forward onto the soft fake grass.

ELECTRIC ARROWS

8

When Keke comes to, she's lying in a white swing bed in what looks like a sanitarium. She blinks at the bright white lights above her, trying to piece together what happened, where she is, and why her upper back is aching as if she's been hit by an ice truck.

Motherfucker.

A silhouette comes into view, puts a cool, dry hand on her forehead, gives her cheek a rough pat.

"There you go," says an unfamiliar speaker. "Told you she'd be just fine."

There's a buzz of conversation around her, but she can't make out what they're talking about.

"What did you do to me?" Keke croaks, but no one

answers her.

"She was running away," says the surrogate who shot her.

"You did the right thing," says someone Keke recognises. Her face swims into view: It's Mother Blake. Then the psycho surrogate's face pops in too.

"I can't believe you fucking shot me," says Keke.

"Language," scolds Blake.

"You'll be just fine," says the nurse.

"I've just been shot by a psychopath with a bow and arrow and you think I'll be fine?"

"They're just for practice," says Blake. "The electric arrows. They can't do any real damage. We don't use live arrows within the Cloister. Too dangerous."

"It felt pretty dangerous to me."

Keke groans as she sits up, and the bed swings with her movement.

"No more damage than a taser would do." The Surro seems sorry, now. Keke's not sure if it's because she shot her in the first place, or because the arrow didn't do more harm.

Keke climbs out of the bed and winds her arm around her opposite shoulder, trying to check for injuries. Her back is pulsing with pain.

"Barely a bruise," says the nurse. She's not the most

sympathetic nurse Keke has ever met.

She hands her two small paper cups: one with two white tablets in it, the other, water.

"What is this?" asks Keke.

"Paracetamol." Three pairs of eyes watch Keke as she tosses the pills into her mouth and gulps down the water.

Her stomach twinges. "Have you called the cops?"

Blake purses her lips. "We haven't decided about that yet."

Keke shoots her a grateful look.

"That doesn't mean I think you don't deserve to be arrested," says Blake. "I just wanted to give you a chance to redeem yourself."

"I'm listening," says Keke.

"I need you to do something for me."

Now is not the time to be defiant, not if she wants to stay out of the crim colonies. "I'll do anything," says Keke, and she means it. Mostly.

PART II

SCHRÖDINGER DREAM

9

Betty arrives at work slippery with sweat. She has no option but to run to her grind at Propag8 now that the taxi drivers are trying to kill her. She bought an electric car, but they keep trying to boobytrap it. Every time she puts her thumb on the ignition switch she closes her eyes and waits for the explosion. Every time the car starts without blowing up, she knows it's just a matter of time. That she has bought one more day. They are watching her, waiting for the perfect time to detonate her life.

Betty can't handle the daily anxiety, the red-wire-or-black-wire stomach cramps she gets, waiting to be blown to high heaven. Not that she believes in heaven. Not that she believes in anything, except the voices in her head.

So she can't drive the car, but she can't sell it either,

because that would entail meeting up with someone and giving him her bank details. Even if she trusted banks—which she doesn't—she won't want to give those details out to a stranger. She'll have to drive it to an abandoned shopping mall in Fourways and park it there, wipe it down so that there are no fingerprints. No DNA. Because nowadays if you give someone your dynap code, you may as well just hand them everything you own.

Danger everywhere. Can't drive to work, can't catch a ride, so she has to run. Same thing goes for grocery shopping. No wonder she's lost so much weight. Sometimes when she looks in the mirror she is shocked by the haunted skeleton that stares back at her. She probably wouldn't even buy groceries if it weren't for her beagle. It's not the first time the dog has saved her life.

Betty uses her wafer key to get into her office, closes the door behind her, and pulls down all the blinds. She pulls out a few hotwipes to remove the sheen of perspiration she feels all over her body. She scrubs her face and under her arms, and is about to sit down when a male voice crackles into the room.

"Betty."

She shoots up before her pants even touch the chair.

"Yes?"

She's still not used to the disembodied voices of her colleagues beaming into her office like this. It feels as if they can see her every move. As if they are sitting in a control room, like a god, observing her every move. As if she's a cat in a Schrödinger dream.

Is she alive, or dead? She pinches her forearm and welcomes the pain. She's alive. She doesn't know how much longer that'll be true, but today, this minute, she is alive. It won't last long, so it's a bit like being alive and dead at the same time.

She's asked them to refrain from using the Voice Beam in her office, because of her condition, but sometimes they forget. Or maybe they just don't care that she already has enough voices in her head to deal with, without adding staff announcements like *There will be tea and zucchini cake served in the Dahlia Room at 11:00* and *Please don't forget to lock your desks when you leave for the day*, as if she needs reminding. If there is one thing Betty is good at, it's locking up.

"Betty," says the voice again.

"Yes!" She looks round the room, expecting to see hundreds of swivelling eyeballs in the ceiling, staring down at her. She imagines the sound they would make, and she shudders.

"Mandla here. Please come to my office."

"Uh oh," whispers Betty. "That doesn't sound good."

She glances at her snakewatch. Yes, she's late for work again. Of course she's late! Her manager would also be late for work every day if he had to run a marathon just to show up. When she'd told Mandla her problem, he had been understanding. He knew her diagnosis, knew she needed to do things her way. He was—mostly—willing to overlook her compelling eccentricities. But now he's called her to his office, and she doubts it's for a promotion.

Betty knocks on his glass door, and jumps away as it slides open. Her manager looks up with a ghost of a smile. He motions for her to come inside, and the door closes soundlessly behind her.

"Betty." He's friendly, but firm. "Take a seat."

She continues to stand. "You're firing me."

Mandla stops smiling. "I'm sorry."

"I understand. I'm two hours late."

He sighs and his face turns down.

"It's not just about being late. I'm happy to give you the flexitime you need. I just think that—"

Betty stares at him. Part of her wants to put him out of his misery, tell him it's okay, she's glad she won't have to run so much anymore, or deal with insensitive colleagues, or taste the awful office decaf again. The other part of her wants him to squirm. She's given most of her adult working life to this place. She's responsible for the most groundbreaking accomplishments they've achieved, and what does she get in return? A simpering idiot telling her she needs to get help. Because that's what he's going to say, isn't it?

"I just think you need to focus on getting well. Perhaps some additional treatment for your … condition."

"What do you know about my *condition*?"

"I know that when I met you, you were the brightest, edgiest biohorticulturalist I had ever met. You started programmes here that were light years ahead of any other seed storage facility in the world."

Betty stares at him. "It doesn't matter, though, does it?"

He hits the desk with his palm, and Betty jumps.

"Of course it matters!" Mandla says, and he seems to mean it. His face is etched with regret. He sighs and sits back in his chair, resigned. "Of course it matters."

Betty stares at him while her voices whisper in her head. She ignores them.

"You're wrong," she says, and leaves his office.

THE WAFER KEY

10

"Come on, girl," Betty says to the beagle she's dragging on her red lead. The hound's not in a hurry: She's enjoying the impromptu walk, the companionship, the thousand different scents steaming from the hot sidewalk. The beagle looks up at Betty, panting, happy, and Betty softens the line. It's not the dog's fault she's in a hurry. Usually Betty wouldn't bring her out on a mission like this—it slows her down—but the beagle started whining and crying when she was getting ready to leave her flat, which made Betty blanch with guilt. Then she'd felt the presence of some kind of evil, some kind of invasion, and suddenly her home had looked different—as if someone had come in while she was sleeping and replaced all her furniture with exact copies. Her favourite wingback chair looked like the original, it even had the coffee stain on the arm, and the dog-claw scratches on the stained timber legs, but Betty knew it was an imposter. She'd inspected it, even got down on her bony knees to sniff it—which the beagle had thought was a game and joined in—and even the smell was spot-on. How did they get that right? *These creeps ... these creeps are not to be underestimated. These people are very good at what they do.*

Then she'd noticed the painting on the wall—a landscape by a local artist, picked up years ago at the Rosebank Flea Market—looked different, too. The scudding clouds were moodier, and there was something wrong with the shade of the sky.

It's just a matter of time before they get her. Maybe she shouldn't give them the satisfaction. Maybe she should kill herself, first. It'll be better than waiting around like a sitting duck.

Yes.

That is what she'll do, but first she has to warn the others. The envelopes tremble in her hand.

After she'd packed up her box of belongings at work and dumped them into the incinerator chute, she'd hidden the list of barcodes—seven barcodes, including hers—in the fake bottom of a safety deposit box. There's no safer place than a safety deposit box at a seed bank. Now she has three copies of the wafer key that will open it, along with three identical letters, in three separate envelopes, all for the same person. One to speed-post, one to hand-deliver, and one as a backup, in case the first two are somehow intercepted. She clutches the envelopes, and her perspiration makes the paper turn leathery. The beagle spots some pigeons in the distance and barks, straining at the lead, and Betty begins to jog along with her, scattering the charcoal-feathered birds as they go.

She knows what she's doing is dangerous, but the others need to know.

THAT ESCALATED QUICKLY

11

When Keke gets home she has the urge to shower, to wash off the weirdness she's been feeling since visiting the SurroTribe Cloister, since making the deal with Blake, but there's something else she wants to do first. She kicks off her shoes, tears off her imposter dress, sits at her laptop in her lingerie, and slides the Xdrive into her machine. She copies every file over, removes the stick, and takes a deep breath. She still can't believe they let her out of there.

What do you expect? says a voice in her head, possibly Kirsten's. *That they'd keep you there, in a Surro Dungeon?*

Luckily for Keke, they had been able to come to an understanding. Of course, they didn't know she had scraped all their data and was wearing it on her shoe. That may have put a dampener on things.

When Keke tries to open a file, it asks for a passcode. She would try guessing but it's one of those roving passcodes that change every minute, and if you don't have the master rover, there's no way you'd be able to get the code. She drums her fingers on the desk while she thinks.

Keke inserts her earbuttons and logs onto the new DNA dating site she's been visiting recently to check her messages. Nothing too compelling. Of course it's their employment information on their profiles she's interested in, not their profile pic or corny bios. She doesn't care less if someone has blond hair or pink, all she wants to know is where they work, and whether they look like they could make a helpful snitch. She scrolls down the messages, looking for a particular profile she had expressed interest in last night.

She rolls her eyes at the messages from random creeps: "Hey Gorgeous" and "Holy Hell You're HOT" and "Show me your tits!". These people were supposed to be a great match for her, DNA-wise, so finding assholes on her wall is always a bit disconcerting.

"Yes," she says to herself as she finds the man she's been looking for. This time she does look at his pic. It's a black-and-white photograph of the late Hedy LeMarr. Maybe he's really ugly, or maybe he's obsessed with LeMarr, either way, it's of no concern to Keke. He's currently online, and Keke needs to turn on the charm if she wants his help.

KK > So you're a Hedy LeMarr fan?

He takes a while to respond. Keke bites her nails.

MM >> Is there any other way to live?

KK > LOL! OK. A serious fan. I respect that.

Another long pause as Keke waits for him to finish typing.

MM >> I want to be honest with u …

KK > Already? Don't you think it's a bit soon?

MM >> Probably.

KK > What are you going to be honest about? I'm intrigued & listening hard.

MM >> I've seen your profile picture. I need to tell you upfront that I'm not in your league. I don't want to waste your time.

Keke is tempted to type *Oh, honey, no one is in my league,* but decides against it. He doesn't know her sense of humour yet. He may assume she's a vainglorious bitch, which would only be kind of half-true.

KK > I don't know about that. I think your profile pic is pretty hot.

MM >> I'm a tech geek. I have a soft spot for kronuts. And I still live with my mother.

KK > Damn! You were being serious with the honesty thing. You DO know that one of the perks of online flirting is that you can mislead people a whole lot before you meet up with them IRL?

MM >> I don't want to mislead you.

KK > Then I'll tell you something about myself, too.

MM >> You don't have to.

KK > I want to. But you have to swear you won't tell anyone.

MM >> Who would I tell? My mother?

KK > I broke into the SurroTribe compound this morning.

MM > You. Did. Not.

KK >> I did. And I stole data.

MM > Shut the front door. I love data.

KK >> But I can't access it. I'm not an expert but I think it's one of those roving passcodes.

MM > Oh, that's a shame. A crying shame. All that data, and no master rover.

Keke laughs out loud. It's a nervous laugh that kind of hops out of her throat. She takes a deep breath to calm herself down, then continues to type.

KK >> So … I don't say this very often, but …

MM > *listens hard*

KK >> I need a man.

MM > *clears throat*

KK >> But not just any man. I need a man who has the reputation of being the best hacker in Jozi.

MM > Ahem. [In Africa, actually.]

KK >> What I meant to say was, I need the nimble fingers of the best hacker in the whole of Africa.

MM > I may just be able to help you with that.

KK >> Really? Really??

MM > Most def. I wouldn't hesitate to put my hands anywhere near you.

KK >> Ooh. I like the sound of that.

MM > Would you like to Zoom it over? I can take a look.

KK >> They're locked. Non-transferable. Can't Zoom them.

MM > If you're willing to let me into your computer I can do it that way. It's an intimate thing. I understand if you think it's too soon. We hardly know each—

KK >> I'll send you an invitation.

Keke copies his link address from his profile and sends him a team-mate invite to access her machine. There's a small ping and his avatar pops up in her top menu bar.

MM > Okay, I'm in.

KK >> Oh, baby! That feels good.

MM > LOL. Stop. I'm trying to concentrate.

KK >> That's what she said.

MM > You're the worst. And by that I mean THE BEST.

KK >> Can you see them?

MM > Holy Hedy LeMarr!

KK >> What? Problem?? Don't tell me. I've inadvertently picked up a self-destruct virus that's going to eat my whole drive?

MM > Nope. It's ...

KK >> Yes?

MM > Um … you've got your dashcam on, and you're … uh … I'll cover my eyes while you switch it off.

Keke looks down at her outfit. All she's wearing is a teal satin and black lace push-up bra and matching scants. The girls are looking pretty good, if she doesn't say so, herself.

KK >> Or I could just leave the camera on. And you could look as much as you want to.

MM > … That escalated quickly.

KK >> You're adorable.

MM > I'm finding it difficult to focus. You're so …

Keke looks into the dash cam, waiting for him to finish his sentence, but it takes too long. She'll have to help him along.

KK >> Goddamn beautiful?

MM > Yes. Goddamn beautiful.

KK >> Unlock the files and I'll show you exactly how beautiful I am.

MM > You don't have to do that.

KK >> I want to.

MM > I mean, I'll unlock the files for you as a favour. No need for any kind of—

KK >> I WANT TO.

MM > I'm Marko, by the way.

KK >> My friends call me Keke.

MM > How do you pronounce that? KEEK?

KK >> No, more like CARE-CARE. Short for Kekeletso.

Keke watches her desktop as the files start spooling open.

MM > There we go. You can access the documents now. There are … wow. Thousands of them.

KK > That was fast!

MM >> I'm known for that. In hacking, I mean, not …

Keke puts some lipgloss on and adjusts her screen so that Marko can get a proper eyeful. She runs a hand over her cleavage, then unhooks her bra.

MM >> Oh.

KK > Oh? Shall we switch to dual cam? Have some two-way action?

MM >> I'm too shy.

Keke takes off her bra and tosses it onto her desk.

KK > I'm not. So I'll just put on a little show for you, shall I?

MM >> SHUT THE FRONT DOOR. I need to check if I still have a pulse.

KK > You're adorable. Seriously. I have a feeling we're going to get along.

***

After getting Marko back for his favour, Keke logs out of the dating site, turns off her dash cam, and gets to work. She tries to ignore her thudding pelvis while she eats instasoy noodles and stares at her screen. Every day, every room, every surrogate. How did they get away with filming them 24/7? What about privacy laws? Then she thinks of Solonne and is sure that the Surros would have had to waive the rights to their privacy, along with their rights to their uteri.

Keke scrolls through the thousands of videos and can't help but feel it's like watching a reality show. What were they looking for? The whole thing gives Keke the creeps.

But she has to put her feelings for the Tribe aside, for now, and concentrate on finding out who planted the poisoned Easter egg. She auto-sorts the video files into chronological order and then focuses on the clips that were recorded during the 36 hours of the attack. Even narrowing it down like this, there are more than two thousand videos to watch.

A Surro is napping.

A sculpture class is underway.

A pair of Surros drinking tea.

A group of Sisters knitting baby clothes.

Oh my God. How do they stay sane?

If Keke was in there she'd be dashing her head against one of those immaculate walls. It's like she can actually feel her brain atrophying just watching them.

Two and a half hours later Keke finds the video of Joni walking in the garden.

Finally!

She pulls an appalled face at the Surro's violent vomiting. Keke's eyes skitter to the half-eaten noodle bowl next to her, and she pushes it away.

Joni finds the pink sugar egg, and Keke watches the rest through a gap in her fingers. Joni picks it up, admires it, seems lost in thought, and then there's a flash and the screen turns white.

It takes her another eleven hours to find the video she needs. By this stage, she's nearly drooling at her touchpad, her brain is so dead, and she won't be surprised if her eyes are bleeding. Her back is on fire, but it doesn't matter. Nothing matters except the clip she is replaying over and over.

She calls Kirsten, who picks up immediately.

"You're not going to fucking believe this."

"Hello to you, too," snarks Kirsten.

"I have two words to say to you."

"I can't wait to hear them."

"Inside. Job."

"What? I have no idea what you're talking about."

"The attack on the Sigma surrogate. *They* did it."

"Who's *they*?"

"Someone in the SurroTribe."

"That doesn't make any sense," says Kirsten.

"I know! But I've got proof."

"I'm listening."

"I've got the video of the egg being placed on that path."

"Impossible. How?"

"You underestimate my mad sleuthing skills," says Keke.

"Still. Impossible. Unless you … unless you broke in. But that's impossible. Everyone knows it's impossible. Jesus Christ, Keke, did you break in? Do you know what the minimum sentence is for—"

"It was worth it, though."

"You must really want this fucking story."

"Of course I want this fucking story! It's going to be the story of the year!"

Kirsten tuts in exasperation.

"You shouldn't have done it, Keke. Too risky!" She sounds angry.

"I know, but—"

"But, nothing! You know those rumours we've heard …about what happens in the crim colonies. I wouldn't be able to handle you being locked up—"

"Look—"

"Don't tell me to look! Breaking into the clinic is one thing, but—"

"All I was going to say was—"

"What?!"

"Can we argue about this over a drink?"

"I can be there in twenty minutes."

CHRIST ON A CRACKER

12

"It's still not adding up. Why would someone in the SurroTribe want to hurt a fellow surrogate?"

Keke, eyes liquid after a crazy long day and her third whisky, shrugs. "Because people are shit?"

"But they're all supposed to be beyond reproach. They screen the bejaysus out of the applicants and only accept, like, the top one percent. Surros are supposed to be morally, intellectually, physically superior, right?"

"Well, that's what their PR company spins, anyway," says Keke.

"And we all know that PR companies have pants on fire."

"Fake News Central."

"Exactly. Bodum-Sentori was in the news last week for

distributing a fake video. They literally generated a 4DHD clip with Boss Banana handing out food donations in Texas."

"Let me guess, Boss Banana's never even been to Texas."

"Correct. They just photomanipped some other poor schmuck's video. Replaced his head with Boss's."

Keke clicks her tongue. "Some people have no shame."

"What do you expect," asks Kirsten, "with a name like Boss Banana?"

Keke cackles. "True."

They sigh together.

"How are we supposed to believe anything anymore?"

"But that's the thing," says Keke. "I know you're throwing shade on me for being too ambitious—"

"For being *reckless*," interjects Kirsten. "There is a difference."

"Whatevs, but I'm not just doing it for my career, you know. I dig for the truth because it's important. Because it's who I am. Because if we don't have the truth then what do we have?"

"Okay," says Kirsten, pouring another drink. "Okay. I get it. I'll stop scolding you, for now."

Keke looks at the ceiling and mouths an exaggerated *thank you.*

"So are you saying that one surrogate had it in for Joni, or that the whole SurroTribe is behind it? Trying to get rid of her, for some reason? Because, you know, I've always had a weird feeling about those people."

Tumbler in hand, Keke points her finger at Kirsten. "I know, right? Very cultish. It felt so weird being in there."

"I think it's the whole purity thing. Like, they're obsessed with the concept of innocence."

"I guess it's good for business."

"That's probably what it comes down to."

"It makes me feel uncomfortable, too, but I can see why they do it."

"I know." Kirsten crosses her arms and looks at the ceiling. "If someone was going to carry my unborn baby for nine months I'd want to make sure they're not a crack addict with tendencies for dirty sex with strangers."

"Exactly. Also, the epigenetics thing."

"God, yes."

"If the surrogates do pass on their biomarkers in any way, you want good ones."

"The best ones."

Keke lets out a big sigh and sips her drink. Blinks her scratchy eyes as if to clear them. "It's all a fucking trap, I tell you."

"What is?"

"This whole procreation malarkey. From the very beginning it's like you're a slave to that kid."

"That's a bit melodramatic, don't you think?"

"Seriously. It's like you have this compulsion to give your kid the best of everything, all the time. That is *not* a recipe for happiness."

"And you have this magic recipe, oh Wise One?"

"Nope, but I know what I want. I know who I want to be … and that doesn't include little urchins hanging from my legs, demanding things I can never give them. That's why you won't see me making a mini-me any time soon." Keke swings her legs up onto a nearby chair. "No offence."

"None taken."

"I'm way too selfish, and no way I'd ever be able to be a Surro, either."

"Imagine all that dirty sex with strangers you'd have to give up."

Keke laughs. "Exactly."

Kirsten stares at the dead spiderplant on the windowsill. "Okay. So you have a video of a white drone delivering the bomb."

"Not just a white drone. A Surro drone."

"Still. It's hardly conclusive proof, is it?"

"It is, though. I'll tell you why. No alien drones are allowed in the Surrogate airspace. They get shot down by the autodetectors. Ask any pirate paparazzo trying to get footage of the sisters."

"Okay."

"And no one can get into the Cloister compound."

"But you did."

"Ja, but I had a biohacker on my side. I had fucking silicone fingerprints and irises that are so cutting edge they practically haven't been invented yet. Look, it's very unlikely, right? That's all I'm saying."

"And what I'm saying is that you don't have shit."

Keke frowns and plays with her fidget cube.

Click click click click click.

Kirsten is right.

"The whole cult thing makes me feel uncomfortable too," says Kirsten, "but deep down, I don't think it was them. I just can't imagine they have a motive. Besides, there are easier—quieter—ways to kill someone."

"So … what, then? Someone hijacked the drone, from outside the compound?"

Kirsten nods. "Totally possible, right?"

"They would have to have access to pretty advanced tech to be able to pull that off."

"So, who has access to remote drone-hacking tech—and explosives—and wants to harm an innocent like Joni?"

"I don't think it was personal," says Keke.

"A bomb exploding in your face isn't personal?"

"What I mean is, any one of those Surros could have come across that egg. It's not like it was placed in her room."

"Okay. So a hacker hate bomber who has a problem with the SurroTribe at large. Ring any bells?"

Keke rubs her forehead. Her brain is swollen. She needs to drink more water.

"I think I smell something burning," jokes Kirsten, and Keke throws her fidget cube at her. Kirsten catches it.

Keke senses the answer is close, but it's difficult to think clearly when the world is in such disarray. Lately, in her grind, she finds that even a simple conclusion is difficult to reach, because the path from A to B is barbed with so many distractions. But then a little light comes on.

"Hang on," says Keke, "I have an idea."

She grabs her laptop and searches for any kinds of hate groups or threats against the SurroTribe.

"Well, that was way too easy," she says, swivelling the glass screen for Kirsten to see. "We should have guessed."

Kirsten reads the headlines of the top ten search results with wide eyes, hardly breathing.

"Christ on a cracker."

"You can say that again."

SURROSLUTS

13

"We need some kind of proof," says Keke.

"That might be difficult."

"Not really," says Keke. "I know someone."

"This doesn't surprise me."

"The drone that dropped the Easter egg … it'll have a virtual black box, right?"

"I have no idea," says Kirsten. "I stay away from such things."

Keke rolls her eyes. "Technosaur."

"And proud of it!"

"You shouldn't be." Keke shrugs.

"I just treat technology with the suspicion it deserves. That's all."

"Tech's just going to evolve faster and faster," says Keke, "and you're going to be left behind."

"I don't care."

"You'll be crushed in its path! You'll be compost."

"Again, melodramatic." Kirsten laughs. "But at least you're entertaining to have as a friend."

Keke types a short message to Marko on her touchpad. He pings back almost immediately.

MM >> Hello again, you beautiful thing.

KK > More beautiful than Hedy LeMarr?

MM >> I'll have to get back to you on that one.

KK > It's difficult to compete with the first woman to act out an orgasm on camera.

MM >> Although you did a pretty good job earlier.

KK > I wasn't acting.

MM >> You're the best thing that ever happened to me.

Keke can't help smiling.

KK > We've only known each other for a few hours.

MM >> Immaterial.

KK > I need help with another job.

MM >> Anything for you, m'lady.

KK > If I send you the serial number of a private drone can you hack the black box and let me know who hijacked it?

MM >> I'll try my best.

KK > Thank you! Sending it now.

MM >> Roger that.

KK > Will you let me know what you'd like as payment? I'll be looking forward to settling my debt.

MM >> This one's on me. In lieu of the flowers I wanted to send you today.

KK > Oh, TY! *hearts shoots out of eyes* I'd choose a drone-hack over flowers any day of the week.

MM >> In that case it's pretty clear that we're meant to be together.

Sixteen minutes later, Marko sends Keke the server address of the person who hijacked the Surro drone. *Marcus Aurelius* is clearly a catfish name but it points them in the right direction, because his messy cloud footprint is directly linked to the organisation Keke and Kirsten suspect of the attack: a small hate group masquerading as Christian fundamentalists called the Resurrectors.

Keke draws a sharp breath. She has personal experience with the Resurrectors—a petrifying experience—when they firebombed the offices of Echo.news. Keke, working late, had missed the blast by minutes.

Notorious for their failed mission to ban The Net, the group has since taken to terrorising anyone who 'disrespected Jesus'. The Echo newspaper published a column by a cocky, jaded journo in which he criticised each major religion in turn, from which could be extrapolated that he found anyone of religious persuasion a bit dim-witted. A line about rising-from-the-dead Jesus being a huggable hippie zombie particularly inflamed the group and the next day—*poof!*—the building was razed. The Lord doth smite cocky columnists.

"Affirmative," says Keke. "It's exactly who we suspected."

Kirsten goes white.

"What? Are you sure? How did you find that so quickly?"

"A member of the group left his dirty digital fingerprints all over this thing. Plus, Hacker Boy Genius knows how to penetrate drone boxes."

"Your new best friend?"

"Friend with benefits." Keke feels warmth spill into her pelvis. "He's trending so hard on me right now."

“Funny,” says Kirsten, forcing Keke back into the moment, snuffing out the beginnings of an erotic daydream.

“Funny?”

“Isn’t it funny how religious fundamentalists can’t keep their online identities neat and narrow. How they think the rules don’t apply to them. They think they can get away with anything because they have God on their side.”

“Sociopaths,” says Keke. “Or psychopaths. I never know the difference.”

“I should have guessed it was them when we first heard about the Sigma surrogate,” says Kirsten. “They published a piece on FreeSpeech.za a few weeks back, saying how fertility treatment is unnatural, that it’s the devil’s work, and calling the Sisters ‘SurroSluts’. I think they take particular exception to the fact that most of the SurroSisters are virgins. I mean, there was only supposed to be one immaculate conception, right?”

“Right.”

“And they backed up their crazy ideology with archaic biblical verses. ”

“And you read it?”

“I didn’t get very far. All the exclamation marks hurt my eyes.”

Keke snorts.

“But they’ve never injured anyone before,” says Kirsten. “They don’t believe in hurting people.”

"Thou shalt not kill, right?" says Keke.

"Unless your god tells you to. Then it's okay. Then all of a sudden bombs and guns and knives become God's arsenal."

"Deranged."

"Well, whatever their warp is, you were right."

"About?"

"About this being a huge story. Huge! Well done. And we might even get to save some surrogates."

Keke doesn't smile. Her deal with Mother Blake haunts her, and the idea of the Resurrectors systematically targeting the SurroSisters is nothing short of terrifying.

VR BAR

14

Keke needs to blow off some steam, so she's on her way to the hot (and controversial) VR Bar. She's been driving herself crazy with changing her mind every five minutes about whether she should write the article exposing the Resurrectors as the group responsible for the Surrogate attacks. On the one hand, everyone has the right to know. Plus, if she's being totally honest, she also wants the kudos. She's taken risks to be able to uncover the story, and it would be a damn shame to keep it to herself. On the other hand, she made a deal with that Blake woman to keep quiet. It was a condition of her release from the Cloister, and she's pretty sure if she breaks the deal there'll be a whole lot of shit raining down on her. But why are they keeping it a secret? Surely the cops should be involved? Sure, the pigs are pretty useless at the best of times but—

Keke sighs loudly, and the cab driver glances at her

reflection in his rear smartmirror. She senses he's about to ask her if she's okay, but he doesn't. Probably doesn't want to hear another sob story today. Probably heard enough for a lifetime. Working as a cab driver is like double-duty, she's sure. Driver/psychologist. Like a bartender, hairdresser, or prostitute. There's the work you do with your hands, and then there's the real work: servicing all the creeps who yearn for human connection. A slight shiver runs down Keke's spine. Thank the Net she's a journalist.

They pull up at the entrance, and Keke taps her card on the inside of the door to pay and unlock it.

"Thank you," she says, climbing out, and the driver nods. She feels his eyes on her body: slender, strong, and wearing threads that fit her curves so well they look painted on.

She's no introvert, but there's only so much of herself she can give away without feeling drained. That's one of the reasons she's at the VR Bar. With such an important piece of writing on the horizon, she needs to recharge. She's even wearing the studded stilettos she bought five months ago and has never worn. She loves riding Nina, her motorbike, more than she loves the designer high heels, but she's going to be drinking tonight, so the booze and the stilettos win. She just hopes she won't break an ankle.

The bouncer—a musclebound blonde woman with a buzzcut—lets her in without hesitating, and the cashier waves her through. No need to pay to enter clubs like this if you look like Keke. Some places even let her drink for free. The more attractive their clientele, the more popular their establishments become. Win/win.

Keke's never been to the VR Bar before, so she spends a moment surveying the place. Two storeys, five bars, and a number of dance floors. The virtual reality pods are, Keke assumes, behind the glowing doors dotted around the place. It's like an arcade for adults. She orders a beer from the bar closest to her, from a bartender wearing yellow tiger-eye lenses, and shoots the complimentary ShadowShot he offers her. The smoking blue liquor burns her throat and makes her stomach tingle. Keke takes her beer bottle, dripping with condensation, winks at the barman, and makes her way to a pod.

The free booths have doors that glow in rolling neon colours. As soon as Keke steps inside, the door slides shut behind her, locks, and the lights fade.

"Welcome to the VR Bar," purrs a robotic female voice over the sound system. "Your fantasy is our command."

Keke hesitates. A metal contraption takes up most of the room: shining steel, white pads, sensor beads. It looks like something out of a science fiction movie. Will she get out of there alive? The AI registers her hesitation.

"When you are ready, you may undress and put on the SilkSkin suit."

Keke unzips and peels off her clothes, leaving on her stilettos, then walks across to the smoke-coloured suit and runs her fingers over it. The texture of it reminds Keke of the silicone fingerprints Jasmine made for her, which makes her think of the SurroSisters, which makes her think of the article that's hovering over her. She shakes her head, as if to clear it, as if to tell herself she's here for mindless escapism.

She can debate with herself tomorrow.

Keke has a few more gulps of her beer then pulls on the VR suit and climbs into the pod. The machine directs her with beeping arrows as to where to place her limbs. Once her body is correctly positioned, the top of the mechanism—including a glass bubble of a helmet—is lowered and locked into place, squeezing Keke in its grip, which makes her scared and excited at the same time. It's like being in a body-hugging astronaut suit, caught in a sphere. Her whole body is now under deep pressure, and it feels constricting but thrilling at the same time.

"Are you comfortable?" asks the voice.

"Yes," says Keke, breathing into her glass bubble.

"Your blood pressure is escalating. This is normal for your first TVR experience."

"Okay," says Keke.

"We'll watch something calm until you feel ready to begin."

The glass of the helmet transforms into a screen, upbeat classical music is piped in, and a video of guinea pig olympics begins. Keke watches as the furballs compete in a shopping race, pushing miniature pink trolleys, then a veggie-eating contest.

"That's better," says the voice.

Keke does feel much better. She makes up her mind there and then that not only is she going to write and publish the article about the Resurrectors, consequences be damned, but she'll be back here just for the guinea pig videos.

"Are you ready to begin?"

"Yes," says Keke.

"Please choose your experience."

Six options swivel into view. Action, Adventure, Comedy, Erotica, Horror, Romance.

Keke moves her hand to choose from the menu, and is surprised when her whole arm waves freely despite the feeling of pressure all over her body. She tries to move her legs, and they move freely too. It's an incredibly odd sensation. Keke does a few star-jumps and can't believe how easy they are. It's like being in zero-gravity and extra gravity at the same time, and probably the first and only time she's been able to do star-jumps in stilettos. She bounces on the virtual floor a few times, then chooses 'Erotica'.

Since meeting Marko online (Yesterday? The day before? She's totally lost track of time), she's feeling even hornier than usual. Add the stress of the past twenty-four hours, and a no-frills orgasm will be just what the doctor ordered. The menu twists away and disappears, and a new one appears. It wants her to choose a kink.

Menage, Dirty Talk, V-Card, Billionaire, BDSM, Taboo, Vanilla, Real Life.

Keke's tempted to choose 'Taboo', but changes her mind at the last minute. She taps 'Real Life'.

"A Real Life Erotic Experience means that you will be engaging in activity with a fellow player. Would you like to continue?"

"Yes," says Keke.

"You have the option of seeing each other's real faces and introducing yourselves. Would you like to do that?"

"No," says Keke.

"Please choose your identity."

Keke gets to choose between six different body types, hairstyles, and faces. She considers pretending to be a tall, skinny blonde, just for the fun of roleplaying, but decides against it. Nothing beats being in her own skin. Or at least, a close approximation of her skin, she thinks, as she looks at her avatar. It's unsettling how realistic virtual reality art has become.

When asked for a user name, Keke doesn't have to think very hard. She says the name that's in the forefront of her mind.

"Sigma," she says, and adds a tattoo of the symbol on her hip.

Next, she chooses an outfit, and a milieu (a black latex catsuit, and a cigar lounge). The white box in which she's standing morphs into a classy bar, with dim light, piano music and leather couches. Keke can smell the cigar smoke and leather. She breathes it in deeply as she sits on a couch.

“Someone will be joining you soon,” purrs the speaker. “We are searching for a perfect match.”

Keke’s about to lean back and make herself comfortable when she sees something out of the corner of her eye. There’s a man at the bar, who slowly turns to face her. He’s wearing a hoodie so black it almost makes him disappear into the background. He wears his hair in a fauxhawk, and some subtle smudge on his eyes. He’s so goddamn sexy it makes her forget she’s looking at an avatar. He lopes towards her with unadulterated lust in his eyes, and it sends an electric current through Keke’s body. It’s a turn-on to know they’re both here for exactly the same reason. There’s no need to flirt, to impress one another, to waste time talking. It’s the perfect hook-up. No wonder this place prints money.

He comes right up to her and takes her hand, lifting her off the couch. His touch feels so strange at first, as if he is in the pod with her, separated only by SilkSkin. It’s the strangest feeling, because she expects the suit to dull the sensation of his touch, but it does the opposite. It’s like the material of the suit—whatever it’s made out of—extrapolates the sensation. He runs a finger up and down her arm, and it zips right through her.

Jesus Christ. If that’s what his finger feels like—

Now it’s her turn to explore. She unzips his hoodie and

puts her palm on his chest, can feel his strong and steady heartbeat. Starts unbuttoning his shirt but halfway down feels the urge to tear it off him, so she does, then looks up into his eyes which are flaming gold with desire. With one hand on the small of her back, he lowers his lips to hers, and Keke thinks he will kiss her, and can't help but think how strange it will feel, but instead he goes further down and his mouth lands on her neck, and he sucks and bites her there, and it feels like her panties are melting.

Fu-u-u-uck!

It's so weird and so horny at the same time. She wonders who this person is, wishes she could find him in real life, in his VR pod, and exchange numbers and/or bodily fluids because, holy hell, this is fucking amazing.

He has something in his hand: a bottle of pills branded with a Pharmax logo. He flips open the lid with his thumb and shakes two pills out into his other hand.

Drugs won't work in virtual reality, will they?

Stop thinking. Just go with it. You're safe. Just go with everything.

He puts one on his tongue and offers her the other one. She looks up at him and licks it off his palm.

Ecstasy? Viagra? Blunt? Lobster? She guesses she'll find out soon enough, and she's right. Soon there are hot fingers stroking her neck, her back, her stomach, and a wave of warmth washes over her insides. She groans in pleasure. It's some kind of Poppy. Heroine without the headache.

Oh fuck, she thinks, as he starts nuzzling her neck again. Her body blazes with longing for this dark stranger. As if he can sense her clit pulsing, his hand travels achingly slowly towards it. Keke pushes herself against him. *Yes*, her body is saying, touch me, and his hand lands perfectly the first time, and he strokes her through her catsuit, and her whole body lights up with pleasure and desire. The combination of his mouth on her neck and his fingers down there and the shadowy anonymity of the encounter edges her quickly towards the cliff. Keke takes a shuddering breath.

As if reading how quickly her pleasure is climbing, the man slows it down.

"Not yet," he whispers in her ear.

He wants this to last, but Keke doesn't know if she can stop herself. Already fluorescent lights are coursing through her body like lasers, and every nerve is on fire. She's so close to coming, she can't stop. She groans again.

"Not yet," he says again, squeezing her.

He unzips her catsuit, taking his time, kissing her copper skin as he goes, until she is naked apart from her ridiculous shoes and some futuristic-looking lingerie that leaves little to the imagination. His chest swells with a deep breath.

"My god," he says, his smudged eyes flashing as he takes in her body. "I want to feast on you."

He pulls her bra aside and sucks on one of her rock-hard nipples. Keke gasps with the spike in her pleasure. The man hoists her up and she wraps her legs around his waist. She's wet and swollen; she doesn't remember the last time she wanted someone so badly. He kisses her on the mouth, hot and hard and sweet, then throws her on the leather couch and stands over her, unbuttoning his pants.

Holy holy fuck.

He prowls towards her.

THE DEVIANT

15

"You're a deviant," says the man.

Keke cackles. "I'm not the deviant. *You're* the deviant. And I'm … not complaining."

They lie together on the chesterfield in the virtual cigar lounge.

"Your name," he says, running a finger over the tattoo on her naked hip. "Sigma. Eighteenth letter of the Greek alphabet. The symbol means sum, or standard deviation. It's how I'll remember you. The deviant."

"Has anyone ever told you you're not very good at pillow talk?"

"I can't help it. It's my superpower."

"Pillow talk is your superpower?" Keke laughs. "Forgive

me if I find that difficult to believe."

"Maths," he says. "Maths is my superpower. I see it in everything. It's like an X-ray overlay, even in virtual reality. I see it in your delicious hips"—he presses his thumb to her lower lip—"and your mouth."

Keke takes his thumb into her mouth, sucks it, then removes it to talk.

"Your weirdness notwithstanding, I'll take that as a compliment."

"It was definitely meant as a compliment. You're right, I'm not good at pillow talk. I don't usually hang around long enough. But you … You would make any man want to stay."

"I stole it," says Keke.

"Stole what?"

"The name."

The opportunity to tell each other their real names and exchange contact details hovers around them like a giant moon moth. The thrill, after all, was supposed to be a no-strings hookup, but when there is chemistry like this…

Damn! It was so fucking hot.

The man leans forward and kisses her on the mouth, then points at their dashboard. Their time is up. "Time to go."

She wants to say: *Will I see you again?* but stops herself, and the moth flaps away.

Keke gets home at 2am, sated and still aching. She kicks off her heels and massages her sulking feet. She's exhausted, but she knows she won't be able to sleep, not with all the words for the article running through her head. Best to get them all on the page first, before she changes her mind about submitting the story. Her white tattoo is glowing, so she gives herself a shot of insulin, then flicks on her coffee machine. She makes herself a double, and sits down at her desk with a sigh.

"The Sigma Surrogate," she says to her laptop, and the words appear on the glass screen in front of her. "By Kekeletso Msibi."

A SINGLE WHITE BALLOON

16

Keke finishes dictating the article, then spends half an hour editing it while the birds sing through her window. She's got a feeling deep inside her—a jitter—that this is going to blow a hole in the roof. She leaves the document open on her screen so she can admire it for a few more minutes before she jumps into the shower to wash away the smell of stale sweat and sex and coffee, then gulps down two caps of TranX and a bottle of Hydra. She switches off her phone and programmes her Butler to pull down the blackout blinds and stall her artificial sunrise.

Keke climbs into her cool cotton swing bed and doesn't bother turning on her Dream Recorder. She has a feeling she's going to sleep like the dead.

Something's nagging her. What is it? Has she fallen asleep yet? Yes. Groggy. But she can't tell if it's been ten minutes or ten hours. She staggers out of bed and switches on the sunrise. Pink-yellow sparks and smoke floats into her room, and the birds are back: a soundtrack of their singing, anyway, piped in from her master unit. She yawns and stretches; her mouth is a cottonball. She downs what's left in her bottle of water and pulls on her leathers.

Then she remembers the article, and she perks up. She'll have a bite to eat and take Nina for a spin. Despite the submission link being a click away, Keke wants to hand the piece in personally to the chief news editor at Echo. As Keke gets dressed, she bobs along to the song in her head, her mood climbing, hips shaking.

But when she steps out of her bedroom she stops as if someone's thrown a bucket of iced water over her. A single white balloon floats next to her laptop.

What the—

She stumbles in fright, holding on to the wall to keep her balance.

"Good afternoon, Miss Msibi," says Mother Blake, stepping into Keke's line of vision. There is someone with her. A young man—handsome—with balled fists, and dragon scales for eyes.

Blake takes another step towards Keke, and Keke reverses down the passage.

Blake's eyes drill into her. "It appears you have broken our deal."

***

Keke, shaking, leaps onto her bike and thumbs the ignition.

We just want to talk! Blake had shouted after her as she had grabbed her laptop and hightailed it out of her flat.

That may be the case, thinks Keke, but she wasn't going to take any chances. Why had the senior Surro brought a henchman with her? No way Keke was going to hang around to find out. She'd pressed the panic button as soon as she had seen that spooky white balloon. Her security company can sling them out. No way she's getting into a brawl with Blake or her sharp-fisted minion.

Nina roars to life. They rumble out of the parking lot and into the busy city street, Blake's words echoing inside Keke's helmet.

You don't understand the consequences of your actions, she had said.

Some things need to stay buried.

Your ambition is making you reckless.

People are going to get hurt.

If you publish this story, you'll be putting the surrogates in even more danger.

But wouldn't more people get hurt if she stayed quiet? Wasn't it more dangerous to keep this a secret? If the Resurrectors are upping the ante by hurting people, surely they need to be stopped before they gather momentum?

Keke argues with Blake's voice in her head all the way to the new Echo.news building. Is she running this story for Joni and the Surros, or is she doing it for herself? For her reckless ambition, as Blake had said?

She doesn't know the answer to that, but what she does know is that she refuses to be intimidated, and there's one very clear way to send that message to the Tribe.

Keke runs up the escalator at Echo, an art deco building painted in a pastel green colour that Kirsten calls *pistachio ice cream*, then jogs on the conveyer belt towards Ayanda's office. She gets there out of breath and smacks the button on the glass sliding door of the chief news editor's office. Ayanda looks up at her, pencil-in-mouth, still typing.

Keke pants and holds up her laptop bag.

"I've got a story for you."

BURNT SKY

17

Kirsten is retouching her photographs from the Roller Rink Inc. job. Despite having left halfway through the assignment, she's happy with the shots. Back in varsity, her photography lecturer had told her she had such a good eye that she'd be able to make a dead cat look good, and the comment had revolted and pleased Kirsten at the same time. She does have a knack for photography—always has—but she's often felt that she can't take any credit for it. She's sure it's somehow related to her synaesthesia. It's as if she sees things in a different dimension compared to most people, and she can't explain it, but somehow that comes through in the shots. Her photography is gritty, textured, tinted: deeper than how a regular person sees the world.

When she won the Press Excellence award last year for her work on Somali pirates, she couldn't help but feel as if she had cheated. She had tried to explain her feelings of imposter syndrome to Keke, but Keke didn't get it. Keke was born with a confidence gene. Kirsten's always admired her boldness, and wishes she could emulate that part of her, but unfortunately she's stuck with her own crap personality, so she has to do the best with the hand she's been dealt, which entails, in no particular order: stubborn infertility, crackers cross-wired senses, a big flavourless blank of childhood memories, and what she calls her Black Hole: a gaping hollow feeling where her heart should be.

"Sucks to be me," she says, then pulls herself together. The world is filled with poverty, disease, and every shade of desperation, and here she is, sitting in her cosy flat, working at her $10,000 computer, lamenting her melancholia.

Jesus, sometimes she can't stand herself.

Her snakewatch buzzes, snapping her out of the negative spiral of her thoughts. A spray of powder blue dots emanates from her wrist. It's her OvoApp, telling her that her fertility window opens today. According to her body's signals, she'll be ovulating within the next twelve to twenty-four hours. This cheers her up. At least she'll get laid.

Next, her news tickertape on her curved computer screen lights up with headlines. Echo.news knows which topics interest her most and alerts her to the top stories in her interest spheres. Kirsten begins to wonder how she ever gets any work done, with all the distractions constantly on offer.

Bad boy South African sprinter William Soraya breaks new Olympic record; denies allegations of resping.

Do robots deserve rights?

Billionaire donates entire fortune to charity to live on the street.

One Step Closer to Mars: First commercial passenger ships under construction in Asia.

Kirsten's interested in the billionaire story, so she taps on her glass screen and a video box pops up. She's about to click 'play' when she hears a rustle from the other side of the apartment and almost shoots out of her chair. She's sure she locked the door on her way in. She's sure. Sure enough.

Oh, fuck, did she not lock the door?

Her pulse is a purple ripple in her ears, and a jet of yellow adrenaline spikes her blood. Someone's in her house. She instinctively grabs at her chest to calm her heart, to stop it from ejecting right out of her throat.

Oh fuck oh fuck oh fuck.

Her panic button is on her keyring, which is hanging at

the front door. Does she go after it, or does she hide in a cupboard? But then it's quiet for a whole minute, then two, and by the third, Kirsten has convinced herself that she imagined the initial sound. It could have just been a piece of paper rustling, right? Or an ornament falling. Things move, even in an empty house. The world is not a stable place. Kirsten's always known that danger is closer than anyone realises. Has waited her whole life for it to catch up with her. Perhaps the moment has arrived.

She pads, slowly, senses on high alert, towards the spare room, picking up a knife off the kitchen counter. She's not going to cower. This is her fucking house. No one's going to come in here and terrorise her.

Is she mad? Probably. But a part of her just wants to get it over with. She grips the knife tightly. Her heart is beating so loudly in her ears that can see the pulsing shapes in front of her.

Kirsten steals over to where she thinks the muffled sound originated. She's armed and ready to do damage to the trespasser, but when she inches towards the doorway, she sees it's James. Relief washes over her body, but her heart is still battering away at her breastbone.

She takes a deep breath and lowers the knife. Puts her hand on her chest. "Hey."

James flinches, and turns around. "Jeez. Give a man a heart attack!"

A flash of white disappears into his medical bag.

"*You're* the one who gave *me* the fright. You're supposed to be in Zimbabwe. I was only expecting you back tonight! I almost knifed you with the blade I bought you for our anniversary."

"That still bothers me, you know."

"It was really expensive. I thought you'd love it."

"I do love it. It was just a weird gift for an anniversary, that's all."

"It's made out of metal. That's what a ten-year anniversary gift is supposed to be."

"Precision-cut, razor-sharp metal." James smiles at her. "I had to sleep with one eye open for a while."

Kirsten laughs despite the adrenaline numbing her hands and feet. "You're such a dork."

"Are you … going to put that knife down?"

Kirsten looks at the glinting blade, then puts it on the bookshelf. Just above, there's a beautiful hardbound vintage edition of 'Hansel & Gretel' on display.

"What are you doing here?" asks Kirsten.

"Clinic's almost out of supplies," he says, ruffling his soft blond hair. "Got an early flight. Need to beg some Jozi corps for funding before I go back."

James is a paediatric heart surgeon who looks like an

underwear model. It's not difficult for him to secure funding.

"I mean, what are you doing in the spare room?"

Had it been a paper envelope he was stuffing into his medical bag when she walked in on him? She wants to know. She's nosy like that.

"Ah, nothing," he says, shaking his head and stepping forward to draw her into his arms. He smells like stale bread rolls, hotwipes and hand sanitiser. *Eau de Plane Cabin.* Still delicious, though. Always delicious.

"Well your timing is impeccable." Kirsten shows him the OvoApp notification on her snakewatch.

"Well," he says, "in that case..."

James starts to lift her T-shirt.

"But you just got back," Kirsten says, lifting her arms. "Aren't you tired?"

"Never too tired," he says, pulling off her shirt.

If she had known he was coming home early and there was nookie on the cards, she'd have worn a nice bra. Maybe matching panties. At the very least she would've brushed her hair, cleaned up a bit.

"Let me quickly take a shower," she says.

"Oh, no. You're perfect. I want you just as you are." He runs his fingers through her hair, caresses her scalp, kisses her on the mouth. She unbuckles him, and he pushes her up against the wall.

Kissing James is always orange: different shades of orange depending on the mood of the kiss. Breakfast kisses are usually a fresh Buttercup Yellow, sex kisses are Burnt-Sky, with a spectrum in between of, among others, loving, friendly, angry, guilty (Pollen, Polished Pine, Rubber Duck, Turmeric). His energy is warm yellow-orange-ruby, sweet, with a sharp echo. Marmalade James.

The doorbell rings.

"Argh," says James.

"Just ignore it," says Kirsten, kicking off her jeans. She wants to take advantage of James's unusual spontaneity. "It's probably the feather-duster man."

"On the third floor?"

"Whoever it is, they can come back later."

They start kissing again, and James hooks his thumbs under Kirsten's panties and pulls them halfway down her goose-pimpled thighs. He's going to shag her right here, thinks Kirsten, and warmth ripples down through her body (Lake Lust).

The doorbell rings again, and James pulls way from her with a sigh.

Kirsten turns in the direction of the front door. "Go away!" she whisper-shouts, and shakes her fist. "I'm ovulating!"

James laughs.

Kirsten shouldn't have joked, she thinks, as they realise at the same time that the moment is gone. They give each other a wry smile and pull their clothes back on.

Marmalade goes to answer the door while Kirsten buttons up her pants, her pelvis pounding.

God, a girl can never get a break.

Her snakewatch rings, and she's tempted to ignore it—why can't people just leave her alone?—but then she remembers her mom had called her the night before in a panic, told her they needed to talk urgently, but not over the phone.

VAMPIRE FACIAL

18

Keke's hopped up after briefing her story in to Echo. As she runs down the escalator, she tells herself she's made the right decision, but guilt pulls at her with clammy fingers. Her mind is all over the place, flitting from the memory of the smudged stranger at the VR Bar, to thoughts of Joni's ruined face, to the image of a group of hooded Resurrectors with their signature shiny plastic Jesus Christ masks, to the white balloon floating in her apartment. She needs to climb down from her anxiety, or she'll fall.

She considers taking Nina for a long ride. Hitting the blacktop at 140km/h with The King singing into her helmet. A loop around Joburg, or maybe she should get out of the city for a while: She could be in the Magaliesberg in a few hours.

Who'm I kidding? What the fuck would I do in the Magaliesberg?

Instead she leaves Nina in the parking basement at Echo and goes for a walk. There's that new park nearby, that urban greening project. CityLeaf. A money grab if she's ever heard of one: Johannesburg is already the most treed city in the world.

It's just a way for the Nancies to award overpriced tenders to their friends, she complained to Kirsten.

Let them have their tenders, Kirsten had said. *Rather trees than guns.*

You think we need trees more than guns? Have you been following the aggressive armament of the northern hemisphere?

Kirsten had shrugged. *Let them build their missiles. We'll have air. At least we'll be able to breathe.*

Kirsten's words hover around Keke as she finds the park and sits on a hoverbench. Her heart hammers away. The sky seems excessively blue to her, and the grass is shouting green. It's as if her nerves are highlighting everything in her vision, and making her organs vibrate. Is this a taste of how Kirsten experiences everyday life? It would drive Keke insane. She draws deep breaths while she crests the panic attack, keeping it at bay one moment at a time until it recedes enough for her to be able to think clearly. The sun warms her pine-leather leggings.

The thought that she'd put her own naked ambition

before the safety of the surrogates nags at her. Seeing a bed of irises nearby gives her the idea that she'll send Joni some flowers. Even if it doesn't mitigate the guilt, it may brighten Joni's day as she endures the bare white inside of that clinic room; no friends or family gathered around the bed, no hands to hold. Not a bouquet or a snack basket in sight.

Jasmine picks up on the third ring.

"Hello my FlowerGrrl," says Keke, standing up.

Jasmine speaks in a low voice. "You coming over this evening?"

"This is a business call, I'm afraid."

"Ah. In that case I'll have to put my clothes back on."

"Tease."

There is a moment of silence, of fondness between them. Then Keke hears some kind of machinery working in the background, a whirring and clicking.

"What kind of business?" asks Jasmine.

"A small thing. Can you please send some flowers to the Conxeption Clinic for me? Anonymously? I'll bump you the details and the bank now if you let me know how much it'll cost."

"Ah, sorry, I can't, actually. I'm not at Pollen today. Kale's watching the shop and she wouldn't even begin to know how to make a decent arrangement."

Keke kicks the grass then leans on the trunk of a tree. "No problem. Never mind. It's not important."

"You can try FloristDrone."

"I will. Thanks. Why are you not at Pollen? Working on a new invention?"

Jasmine pauses, then in a low voice says, "I'm undercover, actually."

"Ooh. I like the sound of that. Anything interesting?"

"I'm figuring out how to spin blood to extract stem cells."

"I'm sorry I asked."

"It's actually very interesting."

"No doubt."

"Give me a couple of days and I may have a very … compelling story for you."

"If you're going to drop a story in my lap," says Keke, "at least let me help you. Do you need anything?"

"You've already done your bit. Your last tip-off is the whole reason I'm playing with blood."

"I won't ask whose blood."

"An innocent virgin I slaughtered just for this purpose."

Keke cackles. "I wouldn't put that past you."

"Talking about innocent virgins … how did the Surro

thing work out?"

"Your handiwork was impeccable. Thank you."

A pause in conversation as Jasmine waits for Keke to continue, but when she doesn't, Jasmine doesn't push her. Ever gracious, she nimbly pivots the conversation.

"And while we're still on the topic of those pesky virgins … I thought you'd be interested in this."

Keke hears the whirring of the machinery again.

"This thing I'm doing—or I'm learning to do—is called a vampire facial."

"What the what?"

"Because you take your client's blood, spin it for platelets, then inject it into their face."

"Holy shit."

"And that's just the beginning. It's amazing what people want injected into their skin. And they practically throw money at you to do it. I may take this job up for real."

"Well, if anyone can pull off the sexy vampire thing, it's you."

SNAPSHOT OF SHOCK

19

"Hello?"

The line is dead. Kirsten notes the caller ID.

Mom.

She hears James close the front door and walk back towards her. The sound of his socks over the pine floor is barely audible, but still Kirsten sees a snatch of the sound, like a lightbulb just after it's been turned off. She blinks it away.

"What's the height of irony?" he says, cocky smile playing on his face.

"What?"

He hands her the delivery he just signed for. A bulk box of pregnancy test strips.

"Ha ha," says Kirsten, resisting the urge to facepalm.

"I'm not laughing," says James, and gives her a playful squeeze on the bum.

Believe me, I'm not either.

"Who was on the phone?"

"It was my mom."

Kirsten tries to call her back, but no one picks up.

This gives her a bad feeling. A storm cloud in her stomach.

"Something's wrong. I can feel it. I'm going to see her."

"I'll come with you."

"No, don't worry. You need to go crank for bank." The Net knows she'd love the company—seeing her parents is always so difficult, especially now that her mom has been sliding into early-onset Alzheimer's—but for once she decides to not be selfish. The lollipop kids with heart problems need Marmalade more than she does.

***

When Kirsten arrives at the house, the grey cloud in her belly gets darker and begins to flicker with lightning. Something is definitely wrong. She walks up the drive, and the colour on the walls reminds her of long, difficult days (Slate Sorrow) and tastes like ash. She'd never been close to her parents. Or, rather, they'd never been close to her. She had tried to form emotional bonds with them, but they seemed to live their lives behind a cold glass wall.

"Mom?" she calls, when they don't open the door after she rings the doorbell. Is the lock broken? Has it been forced? She can't tell.

She nudges the bottom of their front door with the toe of her sneaker and it squeaks open.

"Mom? Dad?"

She pushes the door enough to slip inside, ready to walk towards the kitchen, but she stops in her tracks when she gets to the lounge.

Kirsten feels the earth drop away from her. Her colours all bubble and burst and run together until there's a terrible bright lava burning through everything she knows.

"No," she says. "No, no, no."

Her body is a snapshot of shock.

The room has been ransacked. Furniture has been turned over, drawers flung to the floor. A serving table stands open-doored—a wide open mouth—as if it, too, is in shock. On the carpet in front of her lie her mom and her dad, white as wax.

Cadmium yellow courses through Kirsten. She can hear herself hyperventilating but feels too disassociated from her body to control it. Is this really happening? She's not dreaming because dreams taste different to this.

She takes a step backwards and exclaims as she almost stumbles. Her hands shoot out and she holds onto a chair to keep from falling. Big numb feet. Acid sandpaper mouth.

Her mother, unusually pious, has her hands secured in prayer position with a bracelet of black cable-tie. There's a small hole in her forehead, and a big red bloom over her father's heart.

Bang, bang. Bullet in brain, bullet in heart. One to stop thinking, one to stop feeling.

They're both lying on their sides, death-sunken faces resting on the carpet, which is beige and dull apart from the blood stains (Crimson Comets).

The hot bubbling mess hurtles up inside Kirsten now and she can't hold it in any longer. She runs outside and vomits into the dry mulch of the rose garden.

PART III

GHOST CHILD

20

Being at her parents' burial ceremony is surreal to the extreme. Keke holds Kirsten's right hand, and James, her left. An awkward crowd of thirty or so people gather around the twin coffins. *Super-biodegradable,* the funeral director had assured her, as if she honestly gave a fuck. As if she gives a fuck about anything now that her life is as empty as her sad sack of a uterus. What is it about her that repels life? She's like a bottomless pit, a charged magnet, a dark vacuum.

It's like her Black Hole has come alive and swallowed her whole, and swallowed the people she loves too. There is just nothingness, and Kirsten's not sure she can bear it. Today, her colours are gone.

Her parents wouldn't have wanted a conservative ceremony; they were both scientists, after all. Besides, no one has religious funerals anymore, apart from fringe dwellers and evangelical cults. James had found this place and organised the ceremony in record time. He'd done everything while Kirsten lay prostrate in their bed, not wanting to talk or be touched.

It's called a BioDome TreePod burial, although Kirsten hadn't glimpsed any kind of dome or pod. Probably some kind of evil racketeering, she thinks, her bitterness running through every thought like pollution in a stream. They probably just offload the bodies in a burning dumpster somewhere or sell them for parts, all the while hiding behind these bright supergreen 4DHD animations. And gullible people go away believing that their loved ones have been planted with a tree in some giant biodome of goodness when really they're lying on a butcher's block in the back room, waiting to be dismembered.

You have to cry, James had told her. *You can't keep it in like this.*

Fuck you, she wanted to say, but didn't.

It's going to poison you, he said.

He doesn't understand I do not get poisoned.

He doesn't understand that I AM the poison.

The round pedestal the coffins are on begins sinking, and a large circular hole opens up in the floor beneath it, and the ground swallows up its bounty. And just like that, the room is empty of her parents. As if they had never existed at all. A man in a Hawaiian shirt dabs his eyes.

You have to cry, said Marmalade.

He doesn't understand that one of the reasons this is fucking her up so much is that she doesn't even feel the grief. Not really, not properly. Not the kind of grief you should feel if your parents are murdered in cold blood in their lounge.

Yes, she feels sad, for herself and for them, that they didn't even get to enjoy their retirement after being workaholics all their lives. Feels sad that she never really connected with them, not on the blood-intimate level she craved growing up. It always haunted her, but will haunt her more, now. The grief she's too tired to reach for hovers in her peripheral vision. A ghost child blowing phantom bubbles that disappear when you look at them. A smoky wisp of dread. A grey heart that fades to nothing.

HEART-SKIN

21

Keke is sitting next to her best friend, holding her hand. Kirsten has a weird, vacant stare, as if she's not really there. The TreePod director simpers. He's a small, cold man with green veins snaking under his pale skin. Everything about the building is cool and sterile. Keke shivers.

"We'll let you know as soon as the trees are planted," he says. "You'll be able to visit as often as you like."

James had chosen fruit trees; Keke can't remember which.

"I'll be right back," he says, and takes the director aside, speaking quietly. They leave the room. Keke turns her attention to Kirsten.

"So, I know there's no real answer to this, but … how are you coping?"

Kirsten just stares ahead.

"Kitty Cat," says Keke, using her hand to angle Kirsten's face towards her. "Earth to Kitty."

Kirsten blinks and returns her gaze. "Sorry, I—"

"Don't be sorry. Damn, woman. I'm so fucking worried about you!"

"I'm fine."

"You are *not fine.*"

"I am. Really."

The cooled, filtered air wheezes into the room.

Keke wants to say, *Holy shit I can't believe you were the one who found the fucking bodies!* but she thinks better of it. Tries to be more sensitive.

"You don't smell of anything," says Kirsten.

"What?"

Kirsten takes a deep breath and sighs it out. "Usually you're in a cloud of leather and nutmeg. It's a comforting smell. It's one of the things I love about you. Now it's gone. Everything tastes monochrome."

"Are you … on something?"

Kirsten blinks at her. "Yes."

"What?"

"I don't know. James gave me something this morning."

"Another perk of being married to a doctor."

"We're not married."

"Who is, anymore?"

"My parents were."

"That was always weird, wasn't it?"

"What? Being married? Not really. Not for their generation."

"No, I mean...they never really seemed to be that into each other, am I right?"

The question may come across as inappropriate, given the timing, but Keke suspects the honesty will draw Kirsten out. All the expected platitudes, the affected smiles, the clichés, the *Sincerest Condolences,* they don't touch the surface. They bounce off the heart-skin and fall away; they are discarded like damp tissues. But a real question will dig in; there's no escaping sincerity.

Kirsten blinks at her again, as if remembering who she is. "They were so emotionally unavailable. To me, to each other."

Keke nods.

"And it's not like they just drifted apart, you know? I can't remember them ever being close."

"I'm really sorry."

Kirsten grinds her teeth, spins the ring on her finger. "I need your help."

Keke doesn't hesitate to reply. "You name it."

"They won't tell me anything. The cops. Every time I phone they just say the same thing. That it's under investigation and they'll let me know when they have something. But I know they won't. It's like they've closed ranks and they're never going to let me in."

"Fuckers."

"But I need to know. I need to know what happened. *Why* it happened."

"Of course. I'll see what I can do."

There is a wash of pink in Kirsten's cheeks. Keke expects her to start crying, but she doesn't.

THE LIST

22

Betty watches from afar as the funeral party leaves the building. She's sweating, sweating, always sweating, despite the reprieve from the too-hot sun the tree's shade offers her. Her SPF100 is leaking down her cheeks. One day they'll be playing with the weather and the sun will just explode and kill them all.

"What are you doing here?"

The man's terse voice startles her, sending her heart racing even faster than before.

"Jesus!" She coughs in shock, and knocks at her chest with

her white-knuckled fist. "You gave me such a fright."

James doesn't apologise. "You shouldn't be here."

He's wearing a dark suit, an elegant cut.

Betty tries to swallow the dryness in her mouth. A velcro furball of anxiety. "I tried sending Kate the letters. I don't think she's getting them."

"Her name is Kirsten."

"She needs to know."

"No. She needs to be protected from your paranoid delusions."

"Don't you see it? Don't you see what's happening?"

James's jaw muscles flicker under his skin. "Please leave."

"They're closing down the cell!"

James looks around, maybe hoping that no one will see them talking. "I've asked you before to leave us alone—"

"Christ. Can you not hear what I am saying? We're on *the list.* They are going to kill us all!"

"No. Kirsten's parents were killed in a botched burglary."

Betty chokes. "I know you don't believe that."

She swipes at the perspiration that's running down her temples.

"Look," says James. "I know you've been having some ...

health issues."

Betty hisses at him through her clenched jaw. "You've been watching me. I *knew* someone was watching me."

"I haven't been. Propag8 made a statement in the *Science Journal*, that's all. Said you've been granted a medical hiatus. Your work is famous, whether you like it or not."

"Don't try to turn this around."

"I'm not. I'm ... offering help."

"You're going to try to bribe me. To keep quiet."

James shakes his head, ruffles his soft blond hair. His eyes arrest hers. "Please, Betty."

"Betty-Barbara," she says. "Kirsten-Kate."

"Kirsten's been through enough. Please don't make this any more difficult than it has to be."

He turns away from her and starts walking back towards the TreePod building.

"How many, James?" she calls after him.

He stops and turns around. Annoyance flashes on his face. "What?"

"How many people will have to die before you start paying attention?"

DAYTIME LIGHTNING

23

Keke's hurtling towards the CBD. She'll start with trying to find the police report of Kirsten's parents' murder case. Crime scene description, autopsy findings, possible leads. She's already bumped Marko to ask him if he can help. Hopefully he'll say yes. Hopefully they'll meet up soon to test if their real-life chemistry is as good as their cyberflirting. Her stomach tightens in anticipation.

Her thoughts are interrupted by her phone—which she keeps hidden in her bra—vibrating with a message. Her helmet reads it out to her.

Sigma > Hey Keke. You still want that interview?

Keke dictates a reply.

KK >> Is that Joni?

Sigma > I'd be happy to talk to you. I have a lot to say. Will you come right over?

Keke checks the time on her visor display. 14:23. The clinic is ten minutes away.

KK >> 14:30?

Sigma > See you then.

The exchange reminds Keke of the floral arrangement she'd ordered for Joni. She asks her phone to check the progress of the delivery.

Your gift is on its way! says the FloristDrone's progress page. *ETA 14:30.*

Perfect, thinks Keke. *I love living in the future.*

***

Keke arrives at the Conxeption Clinic in a roar of hot tyres on tarmac. This time, as an invited visitor, she'll use the front entrance. She parks and jogs up to the wide steps at the foot of the building. Her phone vibrates in her jacket pocket, and she stops to check who it's from. FloristDrone.

Your gift has been delivered! it says. *14:32.*

Keke looks up, tries to guess which window is Joni's, and as she does so, there is a boom and a bright flash of white and yellow, and the building trembles. Keke gasps and automatically ducks, gets ready to tuck and roll, but there are no more explosions. Smoke streams out of the jagged window frame, and as Keke watches the grey plume wick up to the sky she instinctively knows that Joni is dead, and the article she submitted is the reason it happened.

The knowledge hits her in the stomach: a dirty suckerpunch. The air is knocked out of her lungs. The clinic's fire alarm is shrieking at her, people are already being herded out of the smoking building. They don't need to worry. There will be no more blasts. The Resurrectors have hit their target.

Keke realises the bump she received about the interview

was not from Joni; it was a tactic to get her here. They must have hacked Joni's phone. Did they mean for Keke to die too? Or just to watch?

She thinks of how young Joni was, how innocent, and the pain in her chest makes her wish for a second she had been in that room when the flowers were detonated.

The sirens of emergency vehicles are angry bees in her head. A police car screeches into the parking lot and Keke, still shaking inside, sprints to her bike and jumps on as the flashing blue lights follow her. Keke punches on her helmet, finds a gap, and roars off.

The screaming police car accelerates hard in her direction.

Keke swings her motorbike out of the clinic parking and onto a service road.

"Stop your vehicle," says the robotic voice of the police car's speaker. "Stop your vehicle."

Ah fuck no.

Keke knows when she's been set up, and there's no way she's going to wave a giant white flag if it means being locked up for something she didn't do.

"Pull over now," says the car as it ramps up behind her, but Keke gives Nina more juice and she flies. Another cop car joins in the chase and they try to box her in, but just as they're getting close, she exits the service street and joins the regular road, dodging communal taxis and tuk-tuks and hawkers selling sweating bottles of CinnaCola. Keke ramps up onto the centre island, scattering pedestrians and informal traders as she zips along the turf. Bright orange mandarins spill into the road and FongKong sunglasses go crashing into oncoming traffic. Cars hoot and flash their lights. Keke pulls Nina back onto the road and puts a hundred metres between her and the pigs, then two hundred. Relieved, she slows slightly and glances back for a millisecond, and when she looks forward again a police car appears from nowhere and jumps right in front of her bike.

All Keke's thoughts disappear as her instinct and muscle memory takes over. Her breathing is quick, and cold adrenaline shoots through her veins. Her grip tightens on the handles as she curves around the obstacle, missing it by a whisper.

But there's no time to feel triumphant, because as soon as she's clear of the cop car, she swerves back to stay on the road—but her nerves have made her hands less sensitive—and she steers too hard and her bike wobbles. Keke tries to keep it under control, clinging to it with her whole body and trying to straighten it out, coax Nina like a spooked horse, and as she thinks it's working, there's a crack in the air, like daytime lightning, and Nina spins out from under her, throwing her onto the heat-glimmering tarmac with a crunch.

COPPER SMARTCUFFS

24

Keke stands up, ready to start running despite the shock and pain humming in her bones, but Solaris stands in front of her like a bad superhero, huge stun-gun to match his wide chest.

"Don't even think about it," the detective says.

Keke squints up at him, the sunshine too bright for her eyes, then looks at Nina, lying on her side, her back tyre blown out.

"You motherfucker."

"You were fleeing a crime scene. What did you think would happen?"

"I didn't think you'd try to fucking kill me."

Solaris looks over at Nina. "What? The bike?"

Keke's so angry with him she feels like spitting, like scratching out his eyes.

Solaris shrugs. "It wasn't me who shot it out. One of the over-eager taser jockeys back there did it."

The arresting police officer is rough with her. He frisks her for weapons but when his hands travel towards her breasts Keke shoots him a look that says *Don't You Dare.*

Her wrists sting where the copper smartcuffs bite into her.

"Take it easy," says Keke.

"Easy?" he says, sneering. "Do you think the guards at the PLC are going to go easy on you? Have you seen what those places are like?"

Illegal photographs flash in on her mind. There's no way she's going to a crim colony. No way. She'd rather be another Suicide Contagion statistic than live that life.

"Someone needs to take my bike."

"We'll deal with it."

"Please be careful with her."

He sniggers without mirth. "You'll be lucky if it doesn't land up in the car compacter."

"You wouldn't," Keke says, anger flaring. She runs her tingling hands over her body, squeezing the tender parts, trying to figure out the extent of her injuries. Of course, what hurts most is that Joni is dead, and it's her fault.

"Are you hurt?" Solaris asks.

"What do you think?"

"Stop with the attitude. I'm here to help you."

"Sure you are."

"Seriously."

"You need to come with me," he says.

"No thanks."

"It's not an invitation. You're under arrest."

"Bullshit. Show me the warrant."

"It's pending."

Keke flinches.

Is this really happening?

"You know I didn't do anything wrong."

"All I know is that I've been ordered to bring you in."

"By whom?"

"A friend."

Keke scoffs, "You don't have any friends."

"I didn't mean a friend of mine, I meant a friend of yours."

Keke's head is spinning. *What is going on?*

"Come on," he says. "Come with me and I'll make sure your bike is taken care of."

He pushes her into the backseat of his wailing SUV, and clicks her safety belt into place. His large face is inches away from her own, and she can smell mint and coffee on his breath.

"I didn't do it," she says.

"Hardly an original line," says Detective Solaris, and Keke wants to punch him on his over-sized jawbone. He slams the door and climbs in the front, starts the engine.

"Why would I kill the lead on my story?" asks Keke.

"That's what I'm going to try to find out."

"It's bullshit, and you know it."

Solaris turns to look at her. "There's a lot of hard evidence."

"Come on, Solaris. You're a better cop than that."

They both know that's not true, but desperation has never been an honest business.

"You know it's the Resurrectors, right?"

There's a spark of shock in his eyes, but he recovers almost immediately.

"All I know, Miss Msibi, is that the explosive device came from a gift *you* sent the victim."

"It was a drone delivery!"

"Your order. Your delivery. Your DNA."

What?

Ice water leaks into Keke's veins. "What?"

"You thought the explosion would smoke the evidence? Your DNA was splattered all over that room."

TIN CUPS AND SIGHS

25

The cool air of the interrogation room sends a wave of goosebumps over Keke's skin. At Solaris's direction she slumps down, hard, into the cold metal chair, and looks over to the fourth wall: floor-to-ceiling, non-reflective tinted superglass—and wonders who's behind it.

Keke feels sick. Guilt and terror swirl around her, hardening her stomach, and her fingers tingle with pins and needles. She shivers with cold sweat.

"You don't look very well," says Solaris. "I've arranged for your insulin to be delivered to your cell."

Keke looks up at him. Her defiance slips a little. Why is he being kind to her? Or is it just part of the manipulation? There's something in his tone that makes her pay attention. Is he trying to tell her something?

Solaris casually spins his Tile on the table in front of her.

"We have street camera footage of a petite woman in black leathers bringing down the FloristDrone with a remote, and planting the incendiary device before letting it go again."

"It wasn't me."

"She had a cat-ear helmet on."

"It wasn't me."

"It's not looking very good for you, I'm afraid."

"Of course it's not," says Keke. "Whoever framed me did a bang-tidy job."

"You'll be interested to know that the warrant is no longer pending. Judge Mbete just signed and sealed it, which means you are officially under arrest for premeditated murder."

"This is such bullshit, and you know it."

"Open-and-shut case. Unless you have something to tell us?"

She can't read him. It's as if he's saying one thing, but his eyes are saying something else. His face, when turned away from the glass wall, is saying *don't say a fucking thing*.

Keke crosses her arms in front of her. "I don't have anything to say."

An almost imperceptible twitch on Solaris's face. He

speaks to the tinted wall. "Let the record reflect that the accused is not co-operating."

Solaris rubs his chest and motions for Keke to stand up again. "Let's get you to your cell."

They walk down the corridor crowded with sharp echoes and harsh light. Tin cups and sighs. Solaris waits till they pass the last ceiling microcam before he nudges Keke into a cell and pushes her up against a wall. Keke thinks he'll try his luck and she'll have to knee him in the balls, but then he backs away, giving her some space to breathe, and whispers to her.

"We know you didn't do it."

JAILHOUSE ROCK

26

Keke's mind is racing.

"Who's *we*?"

Solaris takes so many bribes from so many different factions it's impossible to tell whose side he's on from moment to moment. He closes the cell door which clicks its bolt automatically, and disappears down the corridor. She feels relief and confusion in equal measures, but the overriding emotion is grief.

Keke sits down on the dusty concrete screed floor and starts to cry. She doesn't want to; she wants a clear head, but the trauma of Kirsten's parents' murder, the blast at the clinic, the accident, and her knowledge of what happened to Joni hacks at her trembling heart. It all went so wrong, so quickly, and now the surrogate and the baby are dead, and who knows how many others? Nurses, doctors, tea ladies.

Mother Blake is probably dead too. She sobs into her hands until her eyes are soft and swollen, and she has smudge all the way down her cheeks. She takes a few deep breaths to try to calm herself.

On her third breath, her bra starts vibrating, and the quiet cell lights up with music. Elvis. *Hound Dog.*

Jailhouse Rock would have been more appropriate.

Keke fumbles and then quickly slides her phone out of her top and switches it to silent. She has hundreds of messages. Kirsten, James, Marko. The bumps from 'Sigma' have disappeared.

Keke scrolls up to find the anonymous tip-off that started this whole thing. It had been a short, coded message about the blast at the SurroCloister, and where to find Joni. No shock, no emotion, just the facts. Who would have had that information? The snitch had used the name 'Jane Doe', which had made Keke think of cold dead bodies on steel tables with tags around their toes. Perhaps she should have taken that as an omen and left this whole story alone. Too late for that, now. She scrolls and scrolls, but Jane Doe's bump has also disappeared.

The phone buzzes in her palm, making her heart jump.

MM > Hey, worried about u.

MM > U OK?

Keke decides she won't tell Marko about this. She needs to keep it clean. Part of it is the shame she feels for the role she played in Joni's death. The other part is her hard investigative instinct surfacing despite the havoc it's caused during the past twenty-four hours. She needs Marko's help on Kirsten's parents' case and there's no way she's going to compromise that.

KK >> I'm here!

MM > Oh thank / Net! I was angsting out but didn't want 2 stalk u.

KK >> It's been an interesting 24 hours.

MM > On my side, too.

KK >> Wait, what? You found something?

MM > Yes. No. I'll explain when we chat.

A glint of hope. The hardness in her stomach softens.

KK >> I'm changing your avatar right now to HBG.

MM > ??

KK >> Hacker Boy Genius.

HBG > *blush*

Keke laughs. It's a relief to laugh, to feel normal. She feels her grief retreat, if only for a moment.

KK >> Seriously I think I'm a little bit in love with you.

HBG > *blushes so hard he spontaneously combusts*

KK >> Please don't combust. I want you all in one piece.

HBG > You say the sweetest things.

KK >> In the middle of something right now but can we chat tonight, to discuss developments?

HBG > Looking forward to it, m'lady.

A shadow falls across the floor in front of Keke, and she looks up, swiftly covering up her contraband phone. She does a double-take.

"Christ on a cracker," she says. "I thought you were dead."

MAN OF MIRACLES

27

Mother Blake opens Keke's cell door. "I got lucky."

The senior Surro is calm, but her face is as tense as Keke has ever seen it.

"Jesus," says Keke. "That's an understatement if I ever heard one."

"No, I mean—literally—I got lucky," says Blake. "I left the clinic for half an hour to go to the Cloister to get my lucky yellow mug. The mugs at the clinic are too small, I wanted to have my own. I missed the blast by minutes."

"And Joni?" asks Keke, blind in hope.

Blake swallows hard. "Joni wasn't as lucky."

"But maybe there's a chance? Maybe she..."

“I’ve just come from identifying her body.”

Keke’s eyes prickle, and she blows air up over her face to evaporate the beginning of new tears.

“I’m so sorry.” What else can she say? Joni’s death will haunt her forever.

Blake doesn’t seem nearly as distressed about Joni’s murder as Keke expected her to be. There’s something so stiff about her, so matter-of-fact. Somehow this makes something click in Keke’s brain.

“Holy shit,” Keke says. “You’re Jane Doe.”

Blake offers a thin smile, affirming Keke’s suspicion.

“I don’t understand.”

“You don’t need to,” says Blake. “Everything worked out as well as we could have hoped.”

“How can you say that?”

“When Joni was hurt, that day in the garden ... it was the straw that broke the camel’s back. We had to make a difficult decision. We knew we had to take immediate action or the attacks would just continue.”

“Joni wasn’t the first to be harmed?”

“No, but now we hope she’ll be the last.”

Keke closes her eyes, and tries to make sense of what Blake is saying.

"So it was you who sent me that message?"

"By sending you that tip-off about the attack, we enlisted you, without you knowing."

"Enlisted me?" Keke's thoughts jumble together; she can't think straight.

Blake suppresses a bitter laugh and folds her arms in front of her. "Did you really think it would be that easy to break into the Conxeption Clinic? And the Cloister?"

A mixture of shame and anger burns Keke's face.

"We briefed the guard to turn a blind eye and grant you access. We even left the kitchen door open."

"Why?"

"We wanted you to investigate the blast, but not write the story."

"But why me?"

"We've seen your work. Your dedication to the job. Your unflinching commitment to telling the truth. You're smart and hungry, and that's what we were looking for. Plus ... you simply have connections that we don't have access to."

Marko.

"You needed me to hack that drone's black box. Find the bomber's virtual fingerprints."

"Exactly."

"You needed me to uncover the Resurrector connection."

"Yes. Of course, we had our suspicions, but your work confirmed what we were afraid of. We needed hard evidence—leverage—and you gave it to us. You did a sterling job. Until—"

"Until I filed the story."

"Until you broke our deal."

The two women stare each other down.

"Well," says Blake, with another ghost of a smile. "I can't say that came as a surprise."

Solaris arrives at the open door of the cell. "Come on, you two. Time to go."

Keke frowns.

"You underestimate the Tribe's reach," he says.

"The Tribe can't just break people out of jail," says Keke. "They may be afforded special treatment but they're not immune to the rule of law. Bail hasn't even been set yet."

"There'll be no bail. And no hearing."

"What?"

"Actually," says Blake. "There was never even a warrant."

"Blake set the arrest up," says Solaris. "Faked it. She wanted you in here for your own protection. They had to buy some time for Solonne to negotiate a cease-fire."

"Fuck's sake, Solaris. Is there anyone you *don't* take bribes from?"

The detective smirks and shrugs his giant shoulders. He doesn't care. It's all a game to him.

"What about the evidence against me?" asks Keke.

"The evidence against you is real. The waybill, the DNA. But it turns out that there's more evidence in your favour. You know that footage of the person who planted the bomb on your FloristDrone delivery right under a street security camera?"

"Yes?"

"At first we thought it was you. Petite, head-to-toe black leathers, cat-ear helmet. But she didn't count on a private drone cam catching her throwing the disguise into the boot of a private car two blocks away. When she took off the helmet it was clear it wasn't you."

How did Solaris source that private drone footage? Maybe he's a better cop than she thought.

"You saw her face?"

"No," says Solaris.

"Then how do you know it wasn't me?"

"She was white."

Solaris removes Keke's cuffs, and he and Blake escort

Keke out of the back of the police station. The sun is still blazing hot, surprising Keke's cell-chilled skin.

"Quickly," says Blake, hurrying Keke along the uneven pavement, looking from side to side. A familiar Surro in an ivory gown stands guard with a bow and a quiver of ivory-feathered arrows. It's the psychotic Greek goddess from the other day. When Keke hesitates, remembering the bolt of the electric arrow in her back, Blake pushes her forward.

"Don't worry," she says under her breath. "She's here to protect us."

Dragon Scales motions towards the van that is idling nearby, and the door slides smoothly open, showing nothing of the dark interior. Keke climbs up and in, relieved to be in the shade again, and Blake bustles in behind her. But as Keke's eyes adjust to the light, she gasps in shock at the hooded man opposite her. He's wearing a shiny plastic Jesus Christ mask.

She tries to make a break for it but the doors auto-lock. She tries to open them but they don't budge. Fright flushes her body and she balls her fists, ready to fight.

"What have you done?" she says to Blake, her voice rasping with nerves.

Blake's face is hard.

"Don't blame Mother Blake," says the man in the mask. "I

was the one who summoned you."

Keke bristles at the word. No one fucking *summons* her. She ignores him and grabs Blake's arm, digging her fingertips deep into the woman's flesh.

"You work for the *Resurrectors*?"

Blake shakes her head, then shoots a wary look at the man. "No. Never."

"Solonne and I have negotiated a deal," says the man, "and you need to be part of it."

Keke can feel new perspiration seeping through her shirt; her panic scents the cabin.

Blake's eyes are steel. "It's the only way forward."

Keke shakes her head.

No way, José.

"Now, I know your default setting is to be defiant," says Blake, "but I also know that you want to do the right thing."

"You're going to tell me what the right thing to do is? After delivering me to a killer? Fuck you."

Keke's head is spinning. She's overcome by this strange feeling that being trapped in the car is like being in some compact alternative universe that she has to escape, or die.

"I'm not delivering you to anyone," says Blake. "Solonne set up this meeting. She and the Resurrectors have come to an agreement so that no one else gets hurt. Now we need to do the same."

"Come to an agreement with a bunch of religious nazis? No way. You've got the wrong girl."

What if she kicks Jesus in the balls and right-hooks Blake? Will she be able to get out, then? Or she could grab Blake's shining copper pin and use it as a weapon. An eyeball perforator. But she thinks of the Surro guard outside, and Dragon Scales, and grinds her teeth in frustration. They'd never let her go.

There must be a way.

"Our understanding is simple," says the man, "and will ensure we all get what we want."

"I find that hard to believe."

He steeples his well-manicured fingers. "Tell me, Miss Msibi. What is your greatest wish today?"

Keke's dream has been the same since she started informal flash journalism at sixteen. To write the best damn exposé the country has ever read. But today, a different wish trumps that one.

"What I want, you can't give me. Unless you work miracles."

He tilts his head slighty. "Your wish is to go back in time and save Joni and the baby's life."

"Yes." The guilt is still like acid in her body.

Blake nods. "Good," she says. "Good."

"What would you say if I could make that happen?"

Keke barks a short, humourless laugh. "So you're genie, now? Or a time-traveller?"

"Not quite," says the masked man, lifting his hands and moving his fingers as if he has magic gloves on. "But I am a man of miracles."

"Has anyone ever told you that you have a severely unhealthy God Complex?"

"It's simple. We make a pact right now, and Joni and the baby get to live."

Keke whirls around to Blake. "You told me Joni was dead!"

"No, I didn't," says Blake.

"You said you identified her body!"

"I said what I had to say to get you to understand the stakes."

"Where is she?"

Blake breathes deeply, carefully, as if to calm herself without splitting her seams. Keke sees now that it's fear that's hardening her eyes, not anger, or evil.

"The Resurrectors have her," says Blake, eyeing the man in the mask. "They took her from the clinic moments before detonating the drone."

"Oh thank the Net," says Keke, hand on heart. "Oh, she's alive."

Relief courses through her.

"Alive, but still in great danger," says Blake. "They'll kill her if we don't make this deal. And it's not just Joni. The Resurrectors are masters at abduction."

The man tenses.

"What do you mean, they are masters at abduction?" asks Keke. "Have they kidnapped a surrogate before?"

Blake nods almost imperceptibly.

"Oh my god."

Keke realises something with a jolt. "Sigma means eighteen. Joni's the eighteenth surrogate to be—"

Blake blinks slowly, as if to say yes.

Her eyes say: *It's why we had to take action. It's why we're sitting in this car, a breath away from a potential murderer.*

"Why don't people know about this? How did you keep it a secret?"

"The SurroTribe know what the consequences would be if the press were to find out about it."

Blake acts calm, but the chewing of her lips betrays her anxiety.

"Why are you snatching surrogates?" demands Keke. "What are you doing with them?"

But already Keke knows. She's heard rumours about the trafficking of grey-market surrogates. Women with records of drug use or prostitution, with slates not clean enough for white gowns and copper pins. Women who are enslaved for their fertile wombs, giving birth over and over again until their bodies are broken.

Selling surrogates would be the perfect way for the Resurrectors to assert their disrespect for the sisters without doing direct harm to them. Just last month she had heard a whisper in the chat rooms that the Genesis Project was buying grey surrogates for their secret underground lab. Keke hadn't believed the rumour, though. Everyone knows the Genesis Project is just an urban legend.

"Prove that Joni's alive," says Keke.

The rear window slides down, revealing an unconscious Joni lying in the rear cabin. Her chest rises and falls. Dried blood speckles her hospital gown, and her nails are black with it.

"We had to tranquilise her," says the man. "She's a fighter."

The window slides up again.

"What do you want from me?" Keke has no leverage. They all know that she'll do anything to keep Joni alive. She's completely at their mercy.

"All we need you to do is to keep quiet about this. About everything."

"About everything?"

"About everything you know about the Surros."

"Why? Why do you care? You're just going to keep terrorising them, aren't you? Someone's bound to go to the press eventually."

Blake responds. "Solonne and the Resurrectors have called a truce. The Resurrectors will no longer target the SurroTribe. In return, we'll not press charges, and we'll bury the incriminating evidence you secured for us. If we all keep our sides of the deal, the Tribe will be safe, and the Resurrectors won't be prosecuted."

"You're just going to let them get away with this? What about justice? For what they've already done? What about the other seventeen women?"

"Only God can deal in true justice," says the man, and Keke feels like smashing him in the face.

Blake waves him off. "Some things are more important than justice. It's not as black and white as you see it, Keke. There are so many factors at play here that you don't understand. It's an extremely delicate situation. A hair trigger."

"I'm reasonably intelligent," says Keke. "I'm sure I can wrap my head around it."

"Eventually," says Blake softly. "You will know, I promise, but not today. It's not the right time. All you need to know is that Solonne has laid down the gauntlet. If there is one wrong move on either side, we'll be at war."

Keke kicks the seat opposite her in frustration.

"You're making a mistake," she says to Blake. "Trusting them. Letting them get away with this. No good will come of this deal."

Blake motions her head towards the rear cabin. It's an untenable situation; *it's the only way*, her eyes are saying, *if they want to save Joni.*

The man in the plastic mask speaks again. "Your part in the deal is a simple cease and desist. No more articles, no more investigations. Not even a whisper of any of this to your nearest and dearest."

"They have all your friends' contact details from your phone," says Blake, eyes flashing. "If you break your word they won't go easy on you, like I did."

Keke's biggest instinct has always been to expose, to uncover, to broadcast.

"You need to pretend this never happened, or the consequences will be—"

"What about Echo?" asks Keke. "They already have my piece."

"We've taken care of Echo," says the man, and Keke feels a chill. "I have a friend there. It's how we knew you'd filed the story. He can be very convincing when he has to be."

Keke thinks of all the journos and editors at Echo, tries to imagine who the double agent could be.

"Your story never ran," he says. "And if you want Joni to live, it never will."

Keke's fingers curl up into a fist.

"This is our last chance." Blake's eyes needle Keke's. "You need to make this right."

Does a deal with the devil ever makes things right?

But what choice does she have?

Keke looks down at her fists and forces her hands to relax. Her skin looks grey.

"All right," she says. "You have a deal."

EPILOGUE: EMPTY POCKET

"I think I'm a little bit in love with you," says Keke.

She rolls onto her back and stretches.

"You've said that already," says Marko.

"I'm going to keep saying it."

Marko laughs and takes a sip of water. "I can't believe you're here, with me. This man cave will never be the same."

Keke's body is still humming from coming so hard. "Where did you learn to do that?"

"What?"

"That … thing. With your tongue. And your …"

Marko blushes. "I don't know. Research."

"You've hacked the female orgasm, you know that? You are the ultimate hacker boy genius and I'm never going to let you go."

"Wait until you meet my mother. You'll run for the hills."

Keke cackles. "She can't be that bad."

"She's not bad. She's wonderful. She's overbearing. I'm surprised she didn't come in here ten minutes ago, asking if you'd like a mango lassi."

Keke laughs some more. "That would have been awkward."

It feels so good to leave the trauma of the past few days behind her and just relax into the moment.

"You could patent that technique. I feel like I've had a week at fucking Club Med."

Marko's eyes sparkle. "Stop it."

Keke rolls back towards him and sighs deeply. Inhales his skin, kisses him tenderly on the mouth. "Not gonna stop."

Marko runs his fingers along her ribs. "What are these bruises from?"

The contusions are still fresh.

"And why were you so upset when you arrived?"

"It's nothing," says Keke. "You don't want to know."

"I do. I do want to know. I want to know everything about you."

"Not this."

"Has it got something to do with that data you asked me to help you with? From the Surro drone?"

Keke acts cool, tries to hide the flash of dread she feels.

"I was off base there," she says casually. "I killed that story."

"But—"

Keke kisses him again, long and deep. "Forget about that, okay?"

Joni and the baby are healthy and safe, and living back at the Cloister. Keke's not going to say anything to jeopardise that.

"Okay," he says. She can feel he doesn't want to let it go, but he does as she asks. "What about the other one? The police file on your friend's parents' murder? That's so brutal, man. I mean—"

Keke sits up, her post-coital haze evaporates. "You have something?"

"Oh, yes."

Keke whacks him on the shoulder. "Why didn't you tell me sooner?"

"You didn't ask! Plus, you just started undressing and I was just, like—"

"Okay, you make a good point."

Marko blushes. "I've never had a woman in here. Never mind a woman who looks like … you."

"Good god, man, stop wasting time with the compliments! Spill!" Keke's heart races. "What did you find?"

Marko puts on his black-rimmed glasses and pushes the frames up the bridge of his nose, grabs his Tile from the counter. "I don't really know how to tell you this."

"I'm listening hard."

"Okay. So. According to my sources … scratch that. According to every government and private record-keeping and data storage corp out there, your friend—"

"Kirsten," says Keke. "Kirsten Lovell."

Marko pauses. Intensity lights up his eyes.

"Kirsten Lovell … doesn't exist."

***

Betty stands under a silver birch. It's a young tree, recently planted, but it casts enough shade to keep her from the maniacal sun, and the blistering bark is proving interesting enough for her beagle to investigate. It's her first time at CityLeaf. She usually avoids botanical gardens and parks, despite her profession—or, as she has to continually remind herself, her *previous* profession.

Too many strangers, too much open space. It makes her feel so flesh-coloured and vulnerable. A skinned rat. A baby bird thrown out of its nest by a storm. A snail pulled from its shell. How do these other people cope, she wonders, as they skip by her in their athleisure gear and designer superbug masks that match their tin water bottles. How do they not feel the continual oppressive thrust in the atmosphere that threatens to flatten Betty against the ground?

The beagle has sniffed enough of the tree's scent history now, and strains against her leash, almost choking herself, trying to get to the next object to explore. Betty winds the handle of the leather lead tightly around her bony hand.

"Wait," she whisper-scolds, not wanting to give up the shelter of the leaves overhead, or her view. She's watching Kirsten sit on a hoverbench in the kids' playground area. The jungle gym equipment is bright and new, and completely empty of children. Kirsten hasn't moved in twenty minutes, and her face remains blank. The picture spooks Betty, but she can't tear herself away.

Has Kirsten/Kate received the letter she posted to her? If not, surely she got the one she had pushed under her apartment door?

The dog whimpers, lamenting the trove of lost opportunities just out of her reach. The sound skewers Betty with guilt. She's such a good girl, not much of a guard dog, but loyal to a fault. She bends over to stroke her head, scratch her neck, then digs in her pocket for a bone-shaped biscuit, but comes up empty handed.

Empty pocket.

Frustrated, Betty sighs and closes her eyes. Kirsten hasn't got any of the letters, or the keys. If she had, she wouldn't be sitting in an open park like this, presenting herself as such an easy target.

If she'd received one of the envelopes, she would have gone straight to the Doomsday Vault, but Betty knows she hasn't.

She's not received the warnings, and there's no time to send more. Betty will have to approach her directly. This is not what she wanted. The idea makes her sweat, and she wipes the perspiration off her top lip with a bent finger that smells of warm leather and dog skin.

The leaves above her move in the breeze, whispering silver threats. Betty ignores the voices. She has to focus. She has to keep her mind clear.

The way forward is obvious: Betty will have to force her hand.

The beagle strains and lets out a high-pitched whine. Betty opens her eyes again, and Kirsten is gone.

ACKNOWLEDGMENTS

Thank you to my committed and talented team of beta readers: Kim Smith; Mack Lundy; Robyn Ambler and Brenda Helfrich.

Nerine Dorman, thank you for editing, and Keith and Gill Thiele for your proofreading.

Deep gratitude, as ever, to my loyal readers. I wouldn't be able to do this without you. A special thanks to my supporters on Patreon:

Elize van Heerden
Joni Mielke
Claire Wickham
Kriselda Gray
Wendy Durison

I'm so fortunate to have you all on my team.

WHEN TOMORROW CALLS

• SERIES •

1. Why You Were Taken (2015)

2. How We Found You (2017)

3. What Have We Done (2017)

ALSO BY JT LAWRENCE

The Memory of Water (2011)

Sticky Fingers (2016)

The Underachieving Ovary (2016)

Grey Magic (2016)

ABOUT THE AUTHOR

JT Lawrence is an Amazon bestselling author, playwright & bookdealer. She lives in Parkview, Johannesburg, in a house with a red front door.

* * *

STAY IN TOUCH

If you'd like to be notified of giveaways & new releases, sign up for JT Lawrence's mailing list via Facebook or on her author platform at www.jt-lawrence.com

Lightning Source UK Ltd.
Milton Keynes UK
UKHW011835210120
357363UK00001B/188